Better Than Me:

A Novel

Emme Burton

Better Than Me
Emme Burton
Copyright 2013
ISBN-10: 0991500504
ISBN-13: 978-0991500505

Disclaimer: This book is a work of fiction and any resemblance to any person, living or dead, any place, events or occurrences, is purely coincidental. The characters and story lines are created from the author's imagination or are used fictitiously.

Editor: Sharon Korn

Cover Design: Sarah Hansen, Okay Creations.

Author's Photo: Dana Colcleasure

Dedication

To BC, Thing 1, Thing 2 and the Wookie Dog. I love my life in the HOB (House of Boys). Thanks for putting up with the crazy lady you live with.

Better Than Me Playlist
Songs to listen to while reading Biz's story

Brave-Sara Bareilles

Seven Nation Army-White Stripes

Sweet Child of Mine-Guns and Roses

Wake Me Up Before You Go Go-Wham

Sorry-Buckcherry

Breath-Breaking Benjamin

Get Lucky-Daft Punk

I Really Wanna Love Somebody-Maroon 5

Better Than Me-Hinder

More Than Words-Extreme

Dear Agony-Breaking Benjamin

I Miss You-Blink 182

I Knew I Loved You-Savage Garden

Legohouse-Ed Sheeran

Kiss me-Ed Sheeran

Just the Way You Are-Bruno Mars

Marry You-Bruno Mars

Thing for You-Hinder

Still Into You-Paramore

Table of Contents

Chapter 1: NOW-September

I Can Do This. I can . . . SO. Totally. Do This.

This is my mantra. Has been for a couple of months now.

If I just keep repeating it, I'll be fine. If I just keep repeating it, I can push the panic down. If I just keep repeating it, none of last year will matter. If I just keep repeating it, it will be true. But really, it's not.

I said it to myself, once, a little more than two months ago at the suggestion of my counselor. It worked for about 5 minutes. After lots of repetition, now the words just spontaneously show up in my head, whenever my thoughts fly in the wrong direction. That's pretty often.

I am sweating. I hate sweating. I am lugging boxes and suitcases up flights of stairs, because the ancient Disco elevator in my ancient dorm, Lawrence Hall, isn't working. It's been called the disco elevator by all the residents of Lawrence for as long as I've been here and probably long before that. It's because the carpet that covers not just the floor, but the ceiling and walls, is a psychedelic "Pucci-esque" print in reds and oranges and purples from about 1978. The elevator is probably as old as the building—1928. It has a sliding door that is not automatic and an inner gate door that you have to wrench open. On any given day, the elevator can get stuck between the floors for a few minutes or a few hours—without anyone ever pushing the emergency button—hence the aforementioned "not working."

It's my last year of college . . . Fortunately, I made it back. By some miracle, I am still a Resident Assistant (RA), and luckily, I have been assigned to a new dorm. Sure, it's the ancient dorm, not the modern one I was in for the past three years. I am hoping for a fresh start, clean slate to this year. I live in the dorms because it's the only way I can afford to be at Weldon University. Weldon is a smallish, midwestern university in a suburb of a metropolitan city. It has a reputation as a liberal arts college with a strong emphasis in fine and

2

performing arts. I have a scholarship, a grant and assistance from my parents for my education and books, but I have to cover room and board. So I live in the dorms and supervise my peers. I know I am fortunate to have this job. I am a responsible person . . . aren't I? Sometimes being the responsible one, the normal one is . . . I am still trying to figure out what exactly went wrong last year. *So . . . I can do this. I can totally do this.*

As I unpack my extra-long dorm sheets and comforter and make my almost-loft-style bed in my teeny-tiny RA room, which thankfully is single occupancy and has its own bathroom, I ruminate about all the things that went so askew last year. Losing my sense of self, jeopardizing my RA job with seriously bad decisions and oh, yeah, falling in love with a complete jerk. That was the big one that precipitated the "almost job loss" and ... the other stuff. Just thinking about it hurts and causes my eyes to well up. What an idiot I was. I am depending on people to be kind and have short memories and attention spans as I start this year.

Chapter 2: THEN-September-Junior Year

Landing the "Coolest RA Job on Earth" (I know, how oxymoronic), I was assigned as the RA on the all-male floor for my junior year. After being the RA on the all-female floor sophomore year, I had no idea how I scored the guy's floor. I had a reputation for getting good grades and being responsible, as well as being fun. I think the real reason I probably got it was because I was as close to a virgin as anyone knew of at Weldon. While my freshman roommate had gone at it with her boyfriend whenever he came to visit and had been having sex since she was fourteen, I was a virgin until I was one month shy of my twentieth birthday, during my sophomore year. It was a one-shot deal to get it over with, on a freezing cold waterbed

4

while back home over winter break. Marc, the guy, had been very popular in my high school. He was still pretty cute. And since I was partying and really just sort of looking to get rid of my virginity, he fit the bill. So, yeah, I was as close to a virgin as was possible, since that was winter of sophomore year and it was fall of junior and I hadn't pursued any action since that first time. I think the Residence Director caught wind of my newly minted "nun" status and thought I wouldn't get into too much trouble on the all guys floor. She was… (pretty much)...right, at least for the first semester.

I made some good friends on my floor, Charlie and Smitty. Charlie was hot in a skinny, young Johnny Depp way. He had freaking awesome jet black rock star hair that always looked like he just rolled out of bed, he smoked too much and drove a cool shiny white '69 Impala. He was always so laid back and unhurried. Smitty, his roommate, was a photographer and pretty damn good at it. By the end of his sophomore year, he'd already had a show that was well received. As the critic of the group, he kept us apprised of all that was new, hip and artistically worthy of experiencing. A girl that once dated Charlie told me, "Their room smells like sex and sweat socks." My room smelled like microwave popcorn. . . see? . . . almost virgin. I wasn't just friends with guys on the floor. I also knew people from my classes and from hanging out in the Student Union. My best friend was Jules, a transfer student from the Chicago area. Her dad relocated here for work. She had finished her freshman year, found out about Weldon's programs and decided to move with her family to complete her degree. Jules lived at home, but was at school all the time, especially after she met Charlie. Kris and Mel were friends from sophomore year. They had been roommates on the all girls floor. Kris was studying stage management. Mel, film studies. I was surrounded by talent.

We all converged into to this amusing little group that challenged and cared for each other. That fall, I was on top of the world. The only-girl-on-the-all-guy- floor status was working out great. The guys were respectful. They were great about not knocking on my door after midnight for toilet paper. We had some great floor parties, with Charlie always in charge of the music. Give that boy a theme and he would go crazy. It was as if I suddenly had 24 brothers and they all loved to tease me. School work had never been a problem for me during high school or the first two years of Weldon. Junior year classes were a bit more challenging. I spent more time reading

6

and in the library than usual. As a theatre major at Weldon, I am required to gain experience in all the different aspects of the field, not just acting. Some semesters, I'd work in the scene shop, building sets. Sometimes, I'd be on the lighting crew. Even if acting is your focus, like mine, you're not always cast in a role each semester. That was fine by me. I wasn't even sure I was cut out for a career as an actress. I enjoyed the behind-the-curtain production too. So far, I'd had a small part in one play and in the spring musical sophomore year, but this year I was determined to get one particular part. I wanted the second female lead in Picnic by William Inge. I was meant for the role of Millie, the feisty little tomboy that falls for a guy that leads her on and leaves her. He doesn't return her affection. Just uses her to get what he wants. After studying and rehearsing for the audition all summer, I was beyond thrilled when I saw my name on the cast list. It was later ironic to me that I won that particular role. But I am jumping ahead.

Feeling so confident at having so much of my life working in the direction I dreamed, I wasn't actively looking to become involved in a relationship. I just didn't need it. After all, I had the attention of 24 boys without all the boyfriend hassles. Worked for me.

7

Chapter 3: NOW-Still September

I have been back at school a week. I haven't had to repeat my mantra in days. I know why. It's because I am not coming up against anything that brings back memories or makes me think people are looking at or talking about me. This past week has been Freshman orientation, and since I live in an upperclassmen dorm (you'd think we'd get the newer ones, but no—ancient Lawrence Hall has more single rooms, so it's for sophomores and above), I have basically been all alone on my floor for the week. The freshman, live in Merten Hall, along with some transfers and people that can't afford or don't want singles. On Sunday, the upperclassmen arrive, as do most of my friends. Some of them have chosen to live off campus, like Kris and Mel. Smitty's family lives in town so he moved back in to his old bedroom to save money. Charlie is in a single on my floor, so I am his RA again. Hurray! I'll only be down knocking on his door every three minutes for him to turn down his music. Whether he's listening to it or making it, it's always loud. Good, but loud. That rock star hair he has? Well, fits him. He is a music major—vocal and guitar. He has an amazing, distinctive voice with a huge range and can sing opera, but is a rock singer at heart. He is scarily smart, in a non-traditional way. We were in a Psych class together last year and his observations and perceptions were so far from my way of thinking, I learned as much from him as from the professor. I think Charlie has insight into people that is untapped.

Jules is still living at home, most of the time. She got to know Charlie at the end of last year while hanging out with me in the dorms. She texted me this summer to say she and Charlie wound up in a class together. Charlie had flunked something the year before and Jules was playing catch up from her transfer. They started talking after the first class and by the time fall session came around they were attached at the hip. Figuratively. And many nights, literally. I had the feeling

Jules was going to often tell her parents she was "spending the night" with me when really she'd be down the hall with Charlie.

I'm psyched and more than a little anxious to see my friends. Would I seem different after my summer? Charlie and Jules stopped by my room on Sunday to catch up after they had moved, but I wouldn't see any of my other friends until Monday at lunch in the cafeteria. I thought I saw a few people looking at me as I walked through the dorm and checked on students' progress moving in, answering questions and giving directions. If I thought they were looking at me, were they wondering about the incident in the cafeteria that happened the day school was out last spring. Maybe they were, but I just chanted my mantra and tried to ignore. I WAS NOT going to cry over it anymore. I was just NEVER going to make that mistake again.

Every one of my friends is at "our" table. Even though they lived off campus, Smitty, Mel, Kris and Jules are already here.

In the cafeteria, most of the tables are lined up running east-west, perpendicular to a long row of windows. Only our table runs the other way— parallel to the windows. It's like a head table at a wedding reception. We have the best view of the whole cafeteria and what's going on outside. It's not that we are uber popular. We really

aren't. We just sort of congregated there last year as our group of

friends evolved over time. It became our meeting place for meals.

Not breakfast, of course. Those that eat breakfast at all do it at the

coffee stand that is just outside the cafeteria. Sunday, however is a

different story. The cafeteria serves a huge brunch from 10 am to 2

pm. Even faculty, their families and off-campus students come for it.

It's something special about Weldon.

After grabbing my lunch, I plop down next to Jules. "Hi. Hey,

where's Charlie?"

"He's coming…he was stopping to pick something up, "she

says with a grin.

Kris and Mel fill me in about their new apartment. It's near

campus, but not close enough to walk. They only have one car, so

they're talking about how to coordinate their schedules. Smitty's

family lives on the other side of town. I have a feeling sleepovers

could be happening in his case, too. I just wonder who'll take him in.

As I think about Smitty's possibilities, I look toward the cafeteria

doors and notice Charlie. He isn't alone. He's with two guys I don't

know. They all stride up to our table with their trays. It doesn't

11

escape me that every girl at the table stops to take in the view. A couple of girls walking by greet the darker- haired guy with obvious interest and a touch on the arm. I get the feeling they know him. *Well.* I move one seat down away from Jules to make room for Charlie, since he and Jules are a "thing" now. Jules' eyes light up at the sight of him. It's so nice to see my friend so happy.

"Hi, babe," Charlie murmurs warmly into her ear as he sits and gives her a quick peck. One of the new guys looks sort of familiar and sits on the other side of me.

"Hey" he says. *Cute guy, sort of...pretty.* He has dark blonde hair with highlights, styled sort of Zach Efron as Link Larkin from *Hairspray*-ish. You know, just the right amount of product. Slightly tanned skin. Dark brown eyes that smile along with his lips. Charlie turns to me, puts his arm around the back of my chair and points to Cute Guy with his fork. "Oh yeah, Biz , this is Jake."

Cute Guy continues the thought, "Jake Gianni" he says, and shakes my hand. Firm, warm. *Hmmm...a little formal, but okay.*

I respond, "Biz Connelly. I think I've seen you around. You play guitar, right? You played in the band at Springfest."

12

Jake replies with a bit of a smirk, "Yep, that's right…guitar among other things. I've seen you before too." Excitedly interrupting before Jake can say more, Charlie tells me, "He's playing in our band now."

"You have a band?" I ask with sincere interest.

Charlie and Jake go on to explain that they and a bassist named Simon started jamming over the summer. They have been playing with a different drummer every few days, but are looking for a permanent one. They also haven't come up with a band name yet. Throughout this conversation, I feel as if I am being stared at. The other guy that arrived with Charlie hasn't said a word and I haven't really acknowledged him yet. I look up and am immediately pinned down by a pair of emerald green eyes—unnaturally green. Inhaling slightly, I feel a strange zap or buzz in my chest. *What was that?* He is strikingly handsome, beautiful even. He is sitting directly across from me and continues to look at me intently as the guys continue talking about the band. I bob my head as I half listen. *I really need to stop looking at him.*

Pulling my gaze away from those green eyes, I scan the rest of him. He's got thick dark brown hair. It's long. Almost as long as mine. Okay, that's not saying much. Mine is light red and cut in a severe asymmetric bob that stops just at my shoulders on the side, so a lot of guys have hair as long as mine. He has light skin with a slight flush on the cheeks, and a bit of a five o'clock shadow, even though, it's only noon. I glance at his lips, full but not ridiculous, a little pout to them. But what is really making me uneasy, squirmy even, are those eyes—so green surrounded by dark lashes. Lashes so thick it looks like he is wearing "guyliner." I am almost tempted to ask him if he is wearing contacts. And eyeliner.

"Hey, I'm Davis." He gives me an up-nod and makes no move to shake my hand. I wonder what it would feel like to shake his hand, if just looking at his eyes has me so distracted. It's as if he is looking right into me. *You can do this. You can do this. Wow, I didn't realize I was that anxious, that I had to whip out the mantra.*

"Hi. Biz. Biz Con---" I don't get to finish my name when Guyliner interrupts me, while gesturing at me with a pointing wave of his hand.

"You're that girl," he says, narrowing his eyes.

"What girl?" I ask. *Oh God, does this guy already know all about me? Great.*

14

"The girl from the picture in Charlie's room. The one where you are on a country road and it looks like you've jumped on him and you're hugging him."

I know the picture he is talking about. Thank god, he knows me from the picture, not my reputation.

"That's you?" Jake pops into the conversation.

"Yes, it is."

"You're prettier than in the picture," Jake says.

I don't know quite how to respond to that so I reply, "I'm not sure but I think that might be an insult to me, or maybe the photographer." I point down the table at Smitty.

Smitty has been listening from the other end of the table and hollers down, raising his hand and then pointing at himself in one smooth gesture, "That would be me, so watch what you say."

Jake mumbles in embarrassment, "That didn't come out right. You look great in the picture, but even better in person." Fairly sure my face has blushed bright red, I think, *Thank you*, but I swallow instead and duck my head, nothing comes out. *Jake is so friendly. I'm so on guard, I forgot someone could be genuinely friendly.*

15

I hear a scraping sound as Davis pushes his chair back from the table and leans back in it. As I pick my gaze up from the table and the embarrassment wanes, I think I hear Davis say under his breath something that sounds like, "...both look great," and then shoots a wide heart-bursting smile right at me. He is even more attractive when he smiles. Buzz. Zap. The weird feeling shoots all around my chest and even a bit lower. Disturbingly attractive. I duck my head a little again and turn my head back to Jake, while peeking at Davis out the corner of my eye. *Whoa. This is a lot for a girl who's been in lockdown mode.* Davis stands up with his tray, then drops it a half inch, back on the table. Everyone's head turns to look at him. Smirking, he sarcastically barks, "Sorry." He addresses the entire table. Then just to me he says, "Gotta go." I didn't appreciate how physically imposing he was when he came in. Probably six feet tall at least. Wide shoulders. For the first time, I take in his black t-shirt. It's tight across his broad chest, but what really grabs me is what it says. It has a logo that looks like a parental warning from a video game or CD, which has a large M. Okay, M for mature and then I read the warning part—"May contain: The Guy Your Mother WARNED You About." Okay, so he's cocky. Reading it and thinking about its meaning causes

16

me to open my mouth slightly and inhale. I make a concerted effort not to look lower, since I've obviously already been scanning his chest. He spears me with a gleam in his green eyes and a quirky half smile? Grimace? Turning to leave he tells me, "Have Fun."

Have Fun? What does that mean? Davis appears to have already started to "have fun" before he even leaves the cafeteria. The girls from before have flanked him, each putting an arm around his waist to walk out with him. He whispers in one of the girl's ears and then takes a quick glance back at me to shoot me another smirk. *What?* I shrug it off and turn my attention to Jake.

In the few minutes before I have to run off to my first class of the semester, Advanced Shakespeare, I learn that Jake is a junior, a music major like Charlie and really into Jazz. I like some jazz. We talk briefly about what I know about jazz and I quickly realize my knowledge and taste are limited. Jake isn't obnoxious or pretentious about it. He just chuckles when I bring up the only references I have, Kenny G and Manhattan Transfer. I earn a smidge of respect when I reveal I know that Birdland was written by John Coltrane. Three years of Glee club in high school and a solo on the Manhattan Transfer version of that song left me with that morsel of jazz trivia. I can feel

17

my mood elevating as we talk. This semester could be okay after all.

I look at my watch. I've got to move, and I don't want to be late.

"Hey, it's been fun talking to you but I've got to get to class. See you

around?" Jake nods and gives me a warm smile. He runs his fingers

through the side of his hair where it is shorter.

"Everyone, It's been great. Be good, and if you can't be good,

be careful," I say upon standing, trying to channel the beginning-of-

last-year's Biz. Most of my friends shake their heads and giggle. Jake

flat out laughs. I turn, wave, and am on my way.

***

Walking out of Advanced Shakespeare, I ponder the workload

ahead of me. Dr. Longworth, my Shakespeare professor, is known to

be brilliant and tough and the syllabus proves it. I am wrapped up in

my head thinking about how I am going to balance my assignments in

this class, my other two classes, Film Studies and Linguistics, my RA

gig AND whatever assignment I get in the theatre, when a cold, skinny

arm wraps around my waist and a little cheek lands on my shoulder.

"Whatcha doin?" It's Jules. I wrap my arm around her waist

and give her a squeeze as we walk.

18

"Hi. Thinking about my classes."

"Not Jake?"

"Why would you say that?"

"I saw you two during lunch, sitting next to each other, talking." She says the word talking while making the bunny ears air quotes gesture.

I protest, "Julie Ann, we weren't "sitting together," He just sat down in the empty seat next to me and yes, we were talking, because that's what you do at the lunch table. It would be awkward otherwise."

"So, what do you think of him?" she asks.

"I…what is this? Did you have Charlie bring him to lunch so we could meet? Please tell me you are not setting me up." Jules smiles and rolls her eyes down to look at me. She's way taller than my five feet, barely two inches; five, five when I'm rockin' the heels, which is most of the time. Strangely though, not today.

"I didn't tell Charlie to bring Jake and Davis, but I figured they'd be with him. They have been hanging out together ALL summer, except late at night," she adds in a sexy kitten voice.

"Oh my god, I don't need to know that, Jules."

She snorts a little laugh. "I am not setting you up with anyone. They just seem like good guys and you've had such a crappy spring and summer. I think being with all of us will get you back to the happy-super-fun-to be around Biz."

"I've been a drag, huh?"

"Yeah, a little. I love you. I just want you to be okay." Jules is awesome. She has her own family and love life and shit to worry about and she still thinks about me. I already know some stuff about Jake. Jules fills me in on a few more details. No girlfriend that she knows of. Never seen him with anyone.

"What's the deal with Davis?"

Jules raises an eyebrow and repeats my question, "The deal with Davis? I mostly just know what Charlie's told me—a few facts. I haven't got a bead on him yet. He's older than we are. I think 24 or 25. Transferred this summer from some school in Illinois. He is supposed to graduate in December and then start right in on his Master's in the spring. He's won some mega techie scholarship to Weldon from the Theatre Department. Word is he is this lighting and sound whiz kid. The ladies apparently like him, as you witnessed in the cafeteria. The guys seem to believe he is getting laid every night. Oh, AND he's engaged."

"So it's appropriate a guy like him comes with a warning." I say snarkily.

"Huh?"

Was she not at lunch? "Did you not notice what it said across his chest on his shirt at lunch?"

"Oh, the warning label thing, I get it. Obviously YOU read it, or were you just checking him out?"

"Jules, you know this year is not about that. Any of that."

Right then, I make a decision. It's not difficult. Jules' super spy intelligence on the guys really makes the decision for me. Davis is a player. Davis is engaged. Davis makes my stomach flip. Something about Davis feels dangerous and exciting. I need to FORGET about Davis, no matter how he makes me feel. Between the two, Jake makes me less edgy. I have a feeling we would get along and there would be no danger of becoming obsessive about him. If nothing else we could be friends. I wouldn't lose control. Of the two, Jake is the smart choice.

The only one, actually.

Chapter 4: THEN-Spring Semester-Junior Year

When you've worked with someone for a year and a half and you've never interacted with them other than to say "Hi" or something during a mandatory meeting, you certainly don't expect to be entangled in a life-altering relationship with them that changes you completely.

Neil had worked as an RA with me since I got the job in the fall of my sophomore year. Working as an RA does not mean you become close with all of the other RAs. There were a lot of us: one or two per floor. With two buildings in our complex, one with four floors and one with six, staff meetings were loud and crowded. We had one every week in a small private dining room that you entered through a door off the main cafeteria.

Neil was a person you'd notice. He was strikingly handsome—model handsome—but that wasn't all. Tall, slim and muscular, he had a presence about him that was distant and aloof, to the point of being intimidating. His perfectly groomed black hair and gray eyes, behind an obviously expensive pair of European designer glasses, added to the question mark that was Neil. The entire Neil package put off the message, "I am beautiful, smart and confident, and I know it." Hell, I'd noticed him the first day of my RA training. He didn't notice me.

Honestly, I was a bit puzzled when after a year and a half of almost no conversation and only fleeting eye contact, that at one of our Tuesday evening dinner/staff meetings at the start of spring semester, he pulled out the chair next to me, leaned in really close and said, "Good evening, Biz." I didn't even think he knew my name. I stuttered out a whispered "genius" response, something along the lines of, "Hey." Neil chuckled and proceeded to put his arm around the back of my chair and then focused his attention on our director, Jan Little or Little Jan, as we called her behind her back (she WAS NOT

23

little) as she started the meeting. His arm was warm on my upper back. I willed myself not to wiggle or, god forbid, sweat. It's impossible to will yourself not to sweat, by the way. As the meeting continued and we discussed exciting resident assistant topics along the lines of the number of lock-outs, security issues and toilet paper, the backs of Neil's fingers were lightly grazing my arm. I tensed up. I turned to look at him and he just shot me a closed lip smile and a wink. A wink! What in the hell was going on? I tried to be cool, but inside I was a mess. Neil, hot Neil, was sitting by me and touching me!

When the meeting ended, Neil's arm left the back of my chair. Saying nothing and slinging my book bag over my shoulder, I picked up my tray and took it to the tray return just outside of the private dining room.

"You're on the all guys floor of Merten, aren't you?" I turned quickly to realize Neil was right behind me. I deposited my tray, adjusted my book bag and continued to walk out of the cafeteria, heading to my room.

"Yep, I'm the lucky girl!" I replied with a genuine smile. Neil continued behind me as I walked and talked. *Is he following me?* The cafeteria is located on the lowest level of Merten dorm. My floor is considered the first floor of Merten, even though it's the second level of the building. I've always been a little confused by that. Neil stayed right with me as I climbed the two short flights of stairs to get to the first (or was it second?) floor.

Neil asked, "How'd you get that gig?" *Why is he following me and talking to me?*

"I guess, Little Jan thought I could handle it."

"Looks like you're doing okay so far—might win RA of the year." *Okay, that's it, what is going on.* This conversation is annoying and intriguing.

With my new-found self esteem, I blurted out, "Neil, you have barely acknowledged my existence or spoken to me for the past year and a half. Do you need something? Toilet paper? Are you locked out of your room?" We had been walking down the hall and were now in front of my room. He didn't laugh. He took my elbow and sort of jerked me around to face him. I looked down at his hand on my arm, and then quickly up at him.

His gray eyes darkened and bored into me, "That's not what I need from you, Biz." He came very close and slowly leaned down and kissed me on the forehead. Frankly, I was a bit shocked and just froze there. He closed in and put his hand up on the door frame behind me. "I've been watching you all last semester." *Was I now excited or creeped out?* "You are so hot, I think we should spend more time together." *Whoa, I had never been called hot….ever. Cute…never hot.* He was SO close.

I stuttered, "Uh, okay." Before I knew it, Neil kissed me. It wasn't a "Hey, let's get to know each other" kiss. It was a "THIS is how I want to get to know you" kiss.

He pulled away from the kiss, ran his nose up my cheek until his mouth was at my ear and whispered, "Call you later." The exit to the back stairwell is right next to my door. He was through it before I caught my breath. *What just happened?* I didn't move throughout the entire episode. Well, I moved a little when he kissed me. Mmmmm.

This is the tactic Neil employed over and over. He'd sit next to me at staff meetings, find me in the cafeteria, mysteriously show up right after my classes to walk me to my room. He'd even appear in the study carrel next to me in the library from time to time. Each time we wound up at my door or his door in the dorms. Each time the physical attraction was acted on a little more. I was no longer freaked out. I liked it. I looked forward to it. After two solid weeks of kissing,

26

touching, gazing and groping in states of dress and partial undress, I was so ready to give it up. It was all I could think about during my classes. It was a good thing I was only a dresser for the spring musical and technical rehearsals hadn't started. Some days I could barely remember my name I was so caught up in Neil. I stopped going to the cafeteria and barely spoke to anyone except Jules. Every free moment I had, Neil was there, teasing and distracting me like it was his job.

By March, I'd practically moved into his dorm room. After class or rehearsal, I'd stop by my room to collect things and then go straight to his. I craved sex with Neil in a way I'd never thought possible. I really didn't have much to compare it with. Hell, I was fine living without it after my first experience with Marc a year ago. Now, I would easily skip class to stay in bed with Neil. I got schooled pretty rapidly. Neil liked sex a lot. He was very intense about it. He could just look at me and I would slick up. The physical closeness was something I'd never experienced before. I believed it was a manifestation of how much we cared for each other. We never talked about feelings. Mostly, Neil told me what to do or what he was going to do to me. He wasn't really rough or bossy just commanding. I believed I was with someone that cared about my wants and needs. I spent most of my time with him naked in his bed. He took me in ways I'd only read about in my romance novels and I loved it. I must have been in love with him, right?

During this time, I was called into Little Jan's office twice already for not being around enough on my floor. I'd taken to stacking toilet paper outside my room, so the guys could get some anytime they liked, but the stack disappeared quickly. The other RAs noticed since the guys from my floor kept going to theirs once our stack was gone. Little Jan was really pissed at me.

By mid-April, I had two more BIG RA screw ups. First, there was the fire in one of the rooms on my floor. Microwave popcorn caught fire and the residents tried to put it out by hitting it with towels. The towels caught on fire. The fire department was called, but by the time they arrived, it had been put out. I was nowhere to be found during this debacle, of course, because I was locked up with Neil in his room. A few weeks later, the guys on my floor decided to throw a huge party in the study room on the floor. Study rooms were off limits for parties. It was majorly against dorm policy. They trashed the place and caused enough damage that I had to pay for it with two of my measly RA paychecks. Through all of this Neil was neither sympathetic to my tenuous employment situation nor that I was a target for Little Jan. I was dangerously close to losing my job and he could have cared less.

It wasn't until May that I figured out why. The realization occurred in a none-too-subtle and painful fashion. Evidently, nobody really knew Neil and I were together. I was completely unaware. I thought it was so obvious. Maybe some of my dorm guys might have thought Neil and I were hooking up, but in retrospect, nobody ever asked me about us or asked us to hang out with them. Then again, I had been blowing off spending time with my friends. I was not returning texts or calls. I missed more classes than I ever had in my whole college career. While I was thinking Neil was madly in love with me, something else was in play. I noticed that Neil wasn't walking me places. He was never at the library anymore. He never touched me in an RA meeting like he had before we had sex for the first time. I would wait in his dorm room for hours for him to come back. When he did I was desperate and dying to be with him. He would put me off, claiming to be too tired or needing to study for a test.

I'd made plans for the summer to work summer stock at the University theatre. I would work as an usher or a dresser for some shows and if a small or non-speaking part came up they might give it to me. I couldn't stay in the dorm, so Neil helped me arrange to rent a room from a friend of his that lived not far from campus. I wasn't sure of the rent. I'd slowly moved my stuff in over the past week, so all I had in my room was a backpack with things I needed for the last couple of days.

On the evening of the last day of school, I let myself into Neil's room to find him showering. I thought I heard him sighing, or was it growling? As I walked into the bathroom, he barked at me, "Biz, get out." I was immediately hurt and worried.

"Are you okay?"

"Yes, get out." I backed out of the bathroom and sat on his bed, staring at the bathroom door. He emerged with a towel around his waist. Drying his hair with a second towel he took one look at me and said, "My brother and his wife were just here…..things are getting…complicated with my family." I can't tell if he is sad or annoyed or what? He has no facial affect. I couldn't take my eyes off his wet, half-naked body.

Shaking his head, spraying a bit of water from his hair on me, he told me, "I have really…enjoyed you." And with that he was on me. If he didn't want me for the past few weeks, he was making up for it now. I was quickly without clothes, his lips punishing me. One hand is on my breast, squeezing my nipple almost to the point of pain. His other hand was gripping my ass so tightly I was sure I'd be bruised.

I moaned out a bit, "Neil?" He quickly had me on the bed, but instead of facing me as we usually did, he turned me around so I am face down. He pushed my upper body down onto the bed. I felt his towel slip from his waist. He took me roughly from behind, reaching around to stroke my most sensitive area with little gentleness. He'd never been like this before. Cold. Rough. I was, to my shame, turned on and freaked out at the same time. Both feelings crashed around me as I released in a rush of combined pleasure and pain that I'd never experienced before. It didn't feel right. Why would my body do that, when my head and heart felt so stomped on? Neil came loudly, saying "FUCK ME." He'd never done that before, either, spoken so crudely during sex. I knew it happened. I'd read enough romance books to know, but I didn't like it. Maybe I was just being immature, prudish.

31

I needed to get out of there, but I didn't want to upset him or leave

him. Maybe he needed me like this and he'd been holding back.

Being gentle with the inexperienced chick. My mind was swirling.

He pulled out and quickly threw on his boxers, shorts and a t-shirt.

Grabbing his shoes and keys as he walked out, he said, "Gotta go deal

with that family thing. Lock up, okay. And Biz…. don't be here when

I get back. I've got a lot to do tonight." I was devastated. I lay there

naked, face down, confused and hurt, and cried.

Chapter 5: NOW-September/October

Things are falling into a nice, familiar pattern, sort of like fall of junior year. I'm starting to feel a little less shaky and vulnerable. Classes are going well. The Shakespeare class is challenging, but not overwhelming. Film class is just plain fun. It's a little difficult to stay awake at times in a darkened classroom, especially if I have been up late studying or hanging out. The guy behind me in class nodded off so badly during Citizen Kane that he practically head-butted me. I'd have to say Historical Linguistics is the hardest. It's a bit out of my comfort zone. The reading is challenging, like Chaucer in Old English. Sheesh! I know this is just the beginning of the semester and it will get easier as I understand it more. I just would prefer not to work so hard my last year. I'm working so hard at keeping myself together in general. So, classes: check. We are good there. Self-esteem and anxiety: Not quite yet.

I have been spending time with all of my friends. Lunchtime in the cafeteria is loud and animated as everyone relays their tales of classroom struggles and catches up on relationship gossip. I, for one, am glad I'm not a topic of discussion. Not that they'd gossip about me to my face, but nobody is asking questions and I'm not volunteering any info about myself or others. Jake sits next to or near me every day. He seems genuinely interested in how I am doing. How my classes are going. What's happening on my floor. I learn that Jake is on the 2nd floor of Lawrence. His RA is Suzette, who I worked with in Merten last year. All of my past interactions with her have been positive, so we're cool. Suzette's a Literature major. We've had a few classes together. She's a senior, like me. I've always admired her looks, perhaps because they are so opposite of mine. Suzette looks, well, exotic. Short, pixie-cut dark hair, black eyes and olive skin. Adorable accent. I think she once said her family was from Louisiana. Cajun, maybe? Lately, she's started sitting at our lunch table, down at the other end. That is where Davis sits. Since we were first

34

introduced two weeks ago, Davis hasn't really spoken to me. He always smiles and gives his up-nod or says, "Hey, Biz" with the same gesture of his head, but hasn't engaged me in conversation. Everyday, he always finds a moment to suck me in with those green eyes of his. I admit, I look around for him every time I'm in the cafeteria. I feel a sense of relief once I see him, and enjoy the zapping/buzzing electricity his presence fills me with. It's been two weeks and that feeling is always there. The calm and excitement I feel together are an addictive combination. It's probably a good idea not to get too hooked. I am dealing with it by keeping my distance and reminding myself he is way off limits. But...I can't help looking. If I am throwing off any signals about Davis, Jake doesn't seem to notice.

It's a Tuesday. Everyone's at lunch, and right before we are wrapping up to go to class or back to our rooms to study or nap, Jake reaches over and takes my hand. He's touched me briefly in conversation, but nothing so intentional before. His hand in mine is warm and comforting. Not at all unpleasant. I have been avoiding purposeful touch. Accidental brushes or touches from anyone seem fine, but purposeful touch from a male, I've not sought out. But I am okay with Jake holding my hand.

35

He asks me, right in front of everyone, "Will you come to band rehearsal on Friday night? I want you to hear us. Tell me what you think. There will be a bunch of people there. I think Jules is even coming after she gets off work."

"Ummm…" I stall.

Jules, Charlie, Kris and Smitty start in on me.

"Come on, Biz."

"Bizzy, we haven't been out in so long."

"It will be fun." I agree to go and everyone seems pleased, especially Jake who is smiling broadly. He winks at me and skates his fingers lightly across my palm.

"I'm gonna push this a little further," Jake whispers in my ear. Everyone else has moved on to discussing the Friday night plans and is no longer listening to us. "Will you go out with me Saturday night? To a party, in The Loop."

"Like a date?"

"Not 'like a date.' A date. You'll know a few people there, I'm sure, but it's not only our friends or people from school."

I'm smiling inside if not out. "Sure." I whisper back. I didn't think Jake could smile any wider, but he does.

He squeezes my hand, leans over and kisses my cheek and says, "I'm glad." Jake's attention, his touch, feel…not icky at all. A small wave of relief washes over me. We say our goodbyes until later. Jake leaves after brushing his lips across the back of my hand and releasing it. When I look down the table at my friends to see if they caught any of the interaction, I am immediately struck down by Davis' eyes burning a hole right into me. The expression on his face is unreadable, but his eyes are intense and unblinking. I can't tell what he's thinking. I find myself wishing I could. *Why do I care?* It's not quite anger on this face. It's what? Impassive? Contemplative? No, it's simmering. First, he is looking at me. Then his attention shifts to the back of Jake's head as he walks out the cafeteria doors. *Whatever. It's none of his business. Then why am I concerned?* I stand, gather my tray and bookbag and move to the tray return. As I walk by, Davis reaches up and stops me briefly by gently grabbing my arm at the elbow.

"See you later."

Huh? Whoa. His touch sends a shock up my arm to my chest, causing my nipples to alert and tighten. It feels different than Jake's touch. I try to look unaffected and act like it's not a big deal. Saying nothing, I pull my arm away. I have to do a few things before I go to the theatre.

***

My fall semester senior year theatre assignment is, well, sort of great. I am in charge of the costume shop during the fall season which includes events in an area called The Space and the fall show that will be staged there, Shakespeare's Othello. I am also considered an assistant producer for Othello. Today, I am meeting with Dr. Longworth at The Space. He is the production's Director and Producer. It's dark as I come into The Space from outdoors and as my eyes adjust I can make out two figures sitting on the edge of the stage. It's Dr. Longworth and… Davis. The electricity that I've felt when I've seen him before is right there in a flash. Hum. Zap. He hasn't looked my way or made eye contact and it's already started. It's got to be nerves, I tell myself. I try to push the feeling down and ignore it. *I Can Do This. I Can Totally Do This.* Good old mantra. Davis looks up at me. He raises his eyebrows in a pseudo-surprised look, but it's brief and changes to his smirky half smile. Now I get why he said, "See you later." He knew he'd see me here. Dr. Longworth intones, "Ah, Elizabeth, good, you're here."

"Hi, Dr. Longworth, Hello, Davis." My voice sounds sort of low and, yikes, seductive, when I say the "Hello, Davis" part. Attempting to act cool and not give in to the electrical storm shooting around inside of me, I plop myself down on the stage next to Davis. I can feel the hair on my arms prick up as Davis' proximity increases my shaky zapping feeling. Dr. Longworth chuckles a little and moves to sit in one of the seats in the front row of the theatre. Facing us, he says, "Let's get on with our first production meeting, shall we? Elizabeth, you seem to know Davis. He will be our sound and lighting designer. Phillip Joseph can't be at the meeting today, but he is doing the costume design."

I adore Phillip Joseph. He is a tall, pink-haired costume designer I've worked with many times. "Oh, I love PJ. I can't wait to assist him!" I interrupt excitedly.

Both Dr. Longworth and Davis' faces swivel to look at me, absolutely confounded. Davis gulps out, "He...ALLOWS you to call him PJ? He would normally, in his words, 'cut a bitch' for calling him anything other than Phillip Joseph. How'd you avoid that hissy fit?"

"He loves me," I brag. "We have an understanding. I gave him the nickname. He resisted at first, but when I gave him my

39

reasoning, he was cool with it. I, however, am the only one who can call him PJ." I relay all of this with pride.

Davis is chuckling, "I can't wait to hear this story."

"I'm afraid you'll have to, Davis. We only have a short amount of time to meet." Dr. Longworth halts the digression. "I also still haven't nailed down a set designer for Othello. That's what I'm working on when we are finished here."

We have a general discussion about the upcoming events in The Space and then move on to discuss the production of Othello. Davis has obviously done all of this before, because he is already on top of every aspect. As a matter of fact, HE seems more like the producer than the professor. By the end of the meeting, Dr. Longworth sees that too and basically gives him the job by naming Davis as the co-producer. We wrap up by setting a date for the next meeting. Dr. Longworth says goodbye, leaving Davis and me sitting on the stage next to each other.

Dr. Longworth is barely out the door, when Davis demands I tell him the "PJ" story.

"PJ was the costume designer when I was in Picnic. I've also worked on another couple of shows with him, building costumes in the shop or being a dresser. We hit it off. One night I called him PJ, instead of Phillip Joesph. When I did, everyone around me stopped talking and well, breathing. Like you, they were sure he was going to 'go off.' Instead, he glared at me and said, "Oh girl, why would you call me that?" I asked him did he know what a "PJ" was? His answer was, "something toddlers wear to sleep in." I corrected him. "You see, a PJ is that warm comfortable thing you can't wait to get home and take your fucking pants off for, so you can slip into it and wear it to bed." PJ seemed to like the double entendre of someone wanting to 'wear' him, so he let me keep calling him PJ. I still don't recommend anyone else try it though. Calling him PJ." Davis is laughing out loud and shaking his head. His laugh is full and deep. Real. I've never felt a laugh wrap around me before. I wonder if Davis realizes how being near him has me so alert, attuned to him. He's a sound guy, surely he can hear my heart racing. I tell myself to calm down. This guy is just a work associate. Nothing more.

Davis angles his head toward me and speaks. "So.....Biz? What kind of name is that? Dr. L. called you Elizabeth."

"My name IS Elizabeth. When I was little, Elizabeth was sort of difficult for me to pronounce, I guess. I would call myself

"Bizzybet." My parents, of course, thought it was adorable. They started calling me "Bizzybet," which evolved to "Bizzy. When I was in sixth grade, I sort of rebelled against "Bizzy" saying it made me sound like a bee or something. I asked everyone to just call me Biz. My cousins still insist on calling me Bizzy to this day." All of this comes out very rapidly and excitedly. It's irritating that when I am trying to look my most cool I get the most excited, and I chatter like a squirrel. Happens every time.

Davis gives a short chuckle "I have to say, I've never heard that name before."

"It's different." I agree.

"Much as I like the name Biz, I think I have a better name for you..." Davis has scooted over close and is sort of bumping me with his shoulder. He turns, leans into my ear and whispers hotly, "Elizabeth." I am only hoping he can't sense how much I'm shaking inside and enjoying his closeness. I am waiting for him to tell me some sweet nickname.

Davis continues to whisper softly in my ear, "...sounds like..." And then quickly says louder, "LIZARD BREATH." My mouth pops open in shock, causing him to laugh. I turn to him and sock him on his bicep. He doesn't seem to even feel it. My hand aches. He is much more built than I thought. Davis pops up from the stage, now laughing hysterically and starts running up the aisle. "Lizard Breath, oh my god, it's perfect," he continues, thoroughly amused with himself. I jump off the stage right after him and move up the aisle too, begging "Oh, no, you are not calling me that."

"I am. I love it." He turns and I bump into him chest to chest. ZAP! I back up a step or two. His hands have reached out to grab my arms and steady me, keep me closer to him. He has captured me in his gaze. *Whoa! I want to move closer.* Then I recall that closeness with Davis could be dangerous.

I try to squirm away and inform him, "Fine, then from now on I am going to refer to you as Mavis." Davis makes a face like he is going to protest. Instead he narrows his eyes, shakes his head, mumbles something and blurts out, "Whatever...Lizard Breath is funnier." Grrrrr-this guy is going to be a handful to work with.

Changing the subject abruptly he asks, "What's up with you and Jake?"

"I don't know...we're friends, I guess?"

"Cool. I guess?" he replies.

"A bunch of us are going to the band's rehearsal on Friday. You gonna be there?"

He looks pensive and replies, "I don't know. I mean, I knew about it 'cause I help with their sound sometimes, but I didn't hear about them needing me this Friday." Then he quickly adds, "So does that mean you're not doing anything Saturday night?"

Whoa, is he asking me out or wanting me to work at The Space or what?

"Actually, I'm going to a party with Jake."

"Like a date?" he asks. I laugh to myself because that's the same thing I said to Jake.

"Just like a date."

"Are you with him?" I must have looked at him funny, because he's just staring at me questioningly.

I mumble, "I'm not WITH anybody. It's a date to a party with other people. I don't know, Mavis."

"Mavis....that is classic" he laughs and walks away, quipping over his shoulder, "Have Fun."

Chapter 6: NOW-Still October

Simon, the bassist with Charlie and Jake's band, is thumping

out the opening bass section of The White Stripe's Seven Nation

Army, and advocating loudly for his choice of band names. "I'm

telling you, man, Panty Drop. It's an awesome name."

"I don't know, Simon, we'll put it on the list," retorts Charlie.

"It sounds girlie or pretentious, something. I'm not ruling it out

altogether. We need to keep thinking."

On a short break from rehearsing, the band, along with Jules,

Mel, Kris, and I, are hanging out, kicking around ideas for a name.

The rehearsal space is in the back of a local music store, where Jake

and Simon worked over the summer. It's a funky store that specializes

in vintage guitars. Many touring musicians go there when they are in town to purchase equipment or get instruments repaired. The owner, a well respected musician himself, lets employees use the rehearsal space for free and has taken an interest in Charlie and Jake's band. The space is comfortable, put together with mismatched couches and chairs that look like rejects from Goodwill. There is a large threadbare oriental rug under the instruments in the mocked up performance area. Jake is seated next to me, one hand on my knee, the other holding the neck of his guitar, which is upright between his legs. He is gently rubbing my knee with his fingers. I admit to myself that I like it, really like it. Every time he looks at me I feel a bit more at ease with letting him in, letting him get close. The conversation has gotten a bit heated with each member of the group throwing out a different name or ideas about a name. "It should be a single word, easy to remember."

"Water with Lemon."

"Sounds like an acoustic, granola, hippie band."

"And it's not a single word."

"Lame."

"Are you saying that it's a lame name or the band's name should be Lame?"

The group is getting punchy. The ideas are starting to become ridiculous.

"Ferret Bite."

"Spurge."

"Cougar Bait." Not bad. All the guys in the band would fit that description. Jules and I have a great time teasing them about that name.

"Wait, wait, how about Officer Cox?" Charlie offers.

"Where did that come from?"

Charlie admits, "I got a speeding ticket on Manchester Road one day and I kid you not, the officer's name was Cox. I had to keep myself from laughing when I said, 'Yes, Officer Cox,' for fear of getting hauled in."

During a lull while the rest of the group is quiet, I offer, "How about Charlie's name?" Everyone turns their attention to me. *Whoa, now I'm on the spot.* "I know you guys are a group, but the band was Charlie's idea and he IS the lead singer." They are still listening, but giving me nothing from their expressions.

Finally Jake jokingly says, "Call it 'Charlie's Band'?"

"No, Charlie's last name."

"Boxwood?" Charlie asks.

"Sure, it works for Bon Jovi and Daughtry." I explain.

Charlie seems to be having trouble with the concept. "Boxwood...I've always taken so much shit for that name. You wouldn't believe it."

"I know, I know, but think about it. It's strong-sounding name. It's novel. Separately, and together 'box' and 'wood' are dirty and funny. I always thought the name fit you perfectly Charlie." I'm doing that excited fast talking thing that makes me crazy. *Get a grip, girl.*

"I'm dirty and funny?" Charlie says in a mock hurt voice. Jules is laughing her ass off.

I am laughing, too. "You said it, not me, but yeah."

Charlie pulls Jules onto his lap and thrusts his pelvis, "Dirty."

Jules is still giggling, but enjoying the grinding. In a naughty voice she growls at Charlie, "and funny. Grrr."

There is more discussion. The name is growing on everyone. As they discuss benefits and disadvantages of the name, the guys are setting up to rehearse again, wandering back up to their mics and strapping on their instruments. Drummer of the week, I think his name is Colin, smacks the drum heads a few times. I suddenly get an idea. I run up to Charlie's mic and push him out of the way.

"Ladies and Gentleman, BOXWOOD!" echoes around the room. Everyone laughs. I've always wanted to do that.

The newly named Boxwood is trying to get a bunch of songs together so they can play out. They stick with danceable rock covers like—Welcome To The Jungle, American Idiot and Hard To Handle. I wouldn't mind a few more pop songs, but Charlie has a voice for heavy driving tunes. After another hour or so, they call it a night. Jules and Charlie are going to give Jake and me a ride back to the dorms. His guitar safely packed in the trunk of Charlie's impeccably mantained Impala, he slides into the back seat right next to me, leg to leg, he puts his arm around my waist and pulls me close to him and, putting his lips up next to my ear, says "So glad you came tonight. What did you think?"

"You guys are a fun band. You have got to nail down a drummer, though. People are going to love you."

"You think?"

"Sure, I think you'd be great at a party," I reiterate my approval.

"Yeah, I'm thinking we might stick with Colin. His drumming seems to fit us. Charlie's gonna talk to him at the next rehearsal."

I nod.

"Thanks for helping out with the band name. Boxwood? Never would have thought of it. How did you?" I give some sort of answer about all the ideas that pop in and out of my head all the time and when I say them out loud they either just sound right or wrong to me. It's not easy to explain the way my mind works to another person. I think Jake is listening, but am a bit distracted because he is kissing my neck under my ear and inhaling deeply. All he says is, "Uh huh."

It's a short drive back to Weldon. Once we get out of the car, Jake gets his guitar, slings the case over his shoulder, and takes my hand. We climb the stairs to our rooms. When we get to the second floor where Jake's room is, he doesn't stop.

I remind him, "This is you."

"I'll walk you to your room, if that's okay?" Jake asks.

"Yeah, it's fine." I reply with a small smile.

Charlie and Jules are in front of us. Evidently Jules is sleeping over...with Charlie. Once we hit the landing of five, they turn right to

Charlie's room and say goodbye to us over their shoulders. My room is at the top of the landing. I stop to fish my key out of my cross-body bag. Jake has let go of my hand and has moved his hand to my shoulder. Before I can open the door, he turns me to him and his other hand goes up to my other shoulder. He slowly slides them up and down my arms and looks at me like he is going to say something. Tentatively, he moves in closer, still holding my arms. I place my hands gently on the sides of his waist. He leans in and kisses me. A soft, sweet kiss. Promising, but not pushing. It doesn't last long. My eyes are closed as he pulls away a bit and then, running his nose along my cheek, slides his lips up to my ear and says, "Goodnight, Bizzy. I look forward to our date tomorrow night."

I open my eyes and smile at him, softly replying, "Me, too." Key in hand, I open my dorm room door and step inside. I turn and give Jake a little wave. Once the door is shut, I flip my body to lean against it and rub my fingers lightly against my lips where we kissed. *I can do this. I can do this if it goes slowly and gently, like tonight.* Dr. Matt was right, I moved right through what should have been a panicky moment, using the mantra and knowing that it would be over soon. Even though, if I'm being honest, I was a little disappointed when it was. I sigh and get ready for bed—floating on a little cloud of what feels like hope.

***

I love Saturdays early in the school year. I don't have to rush out to a rehearsal or dorm event. That all changes once the fall theatre productions start. I decided last night when I went to bed that I wouldn't get up early and I would do whatever I wanted today. A little girl time is in order. I want to get my nails done. I might also have Jules trim my hair and help me decide what to wear tonight. It's only a college kegger, but I swear I haven't been out on a real date in years. Probably since I was a freshman. When it gets down to it, Neil never took me on a date. Ever. It was just furtive hooking up. *What was I thinking?* I force myself to stop pulling up memories about that mess and focus on tonight. I am going out. On a real date. With a sweet guy who seems to really like me.

Still in my pink and black Hello Kitty pajama pants and throwing on a black hoody, I pop down to the coffee stand and grab three coffees and a scone. I climb back up to the fifth floor and go to Charlie's room. I hope Jules is still there. She is, still in Charlie's bed. He is up and in the shower. I hand her a coffee and put Charlie's on the dresser. I can hear him singing in the shower. I think it's Sweet Child of Mine by Guns and Roses. This morning, these friends, bring me briefly back to the old Biz.

Jules teasingly admonishes me, "What, no scone for me?"

"Like you'd eat it anyway. I swear you don't eat, even though I've seen you eat. You and Charlie are the skinniest people I know."

"I eat. Just give me a bite." I do.

"You guys are so skinny, it must be like two sticks rubbing together when you have sex. You're at risk of starting a fire." I shoot a smirk at Jules.

Charlie walks out of the bathroom with a towel wrapped around his waist. "Oh, there is no risk, it's a certainty." He winks at me and throws an air kiss at Jules, who giggles into her coffee.

I am instantly red and embarrassed, "I didn't mean to say it like that. . .crap, you know what I meant."

Jules chirps, "Yep, we know."

Changing the subject, I ask Jules if she is free for the day and then turn to ask Charlie if I can steal her away for girl time. She is and he says Boxwood (Hee, hee, he called the band Boxwood) might practice more today, so to go ahead and go do the girl thing with Jules.

Once she is finally out of bed and has said good bye to Charlie, Jules arrives at my room. I've changed into some comfortable yoga pants, a t-shirt and hoodie. Even though it's getting colder outside I wear my black flip-flops because we are getting pedicures and I don't want to wear those flimsy ones they give you at the shop. We snag a couple more coffees and are off on our day of beauty.

I always think I'll switch it up and get a different color of polish, like pink or teal, but always wind up with my favorite. It's a deep blackish plum and has the name of one of my favorite bands in its name-Lincoln Park After Dark. The nail polish company that makes it is known for its original and creative names for their colors. I never have really long fingernails. I can't maintain them, but I love for them to be painted. Jules and I go to my regular nail place, where the owners know me well. I love to listen to their crazy chatter. Because they are speaking in Vietnamese, I don't have a clue what they are talking about. Paranoid as I can be about people talking about me after last year, I never worry about it here. And they could be calling me anything.

Our fingers and toes newly shiny and perfect, we grab some lunch from the deli next door and Jules drives us back to the dorm. Jules is so easy to be around. She doesn't know the entire story of my summer after the episode in the cafeteria the last day of school. She knows more than anybody else, except for my counselor back home, but not everything. Still, I don't feel uneasy around her at all and I'll tell her everything, at some point.

Back in my room she trims my bangs and helps me pick out something to wear tonight. It's between shorts with a graphic t-shirt and a maxi dress and short jean jacket. It's getting a bit chilly for shorts. The shorts outfit is cute and I'm a bit disappointed I can't wear it, but we decide on the maxi dress. It makes me look tall, which is always a goal, but still shows my curves. The jacket is purely for warmth, since the dress is sleeveless. My favorite part of the outfit are my black studded four-inch platform open-toe booties. They scream "rock 'n roll" and make me 5'6". To me, that's practically statuesque. Jules borrows a few things from my closet to wear tonight, since she hasn't been home and doesn't have much in Charlie's room. She can only really borrow shirts and scarves, since she wears tiny size jeans and has much bigger feet than mine.

Hopping off my bed, she tells me she'll see me at the party, blows me an air kiss and leaves. I assume she is going back to Charlie's room. I decide to take a nap, since all major fashion decisions have been made. I want to feel refreshed for tonight. Because, it's Saturday and I have nothing pressing to do and I can.

After closing the shades to my room and turning off all the lights, I slip out of all my clothes except my t-shirt and boy shorts and slide into bed. I look forward to naps when I can get them. Sleep comes easily today. I swear I have just fallen asleep when there is loud, insistent knocking on my door. Crap, I forgot to put out my DO NOT DISTURB sign. I can't believe I have to get up.

"Just a second," I whine.

Opening the door a crack, because all I have on is what I wore to bed, I ask without looking who is there, "What do you...Davis?" It's Davis. He smiles and rakes his killer green eyes over the portion of my body he can see through the crack.

"Are you napping?"

"Obviously, the lights are out and I'm pretty sure my hair is a mess."

"It looks fine to me," he says in a throaty voice and pushes the door open without asking if he can come in. I step back as he closes it behind him. He looks so handsome. He's cut his hair short. When did he do that? He's not in his work clothes. No, he's sort of dressed up, black fitted button up with the sleeves rolled up showing his muscular forearms. Tighter than usual jeans. He's in my room. Why am I not freaking out?

"You look beautiful when you are sleepy, Biz." It's like his warm deep voice is all over my body. He's so close to me, one hand on my hip, as he is sliding the back of his other hand down my face. "So beautiful."

I don't want him to stop. Mmmm, keep touching me. He's pulling me closer. Right into him. I'm still not talking. This is surreal.

He leans in, his green, green delicious stare shifting from my eyes to my lips. Is he going to kiss me? If so, I'm going to let him. I push up on my toes to bring my lips closer. So surreal. I feel his firmness, all of it, pressed up against me. So hot!

It must be a dre…

And with that thought, I wake suddenly. I am covered in a fine mist of sweat and I am touching my own face. My legs are pressed tightly against the pillow between them.

Whoa. It was a dream. A very hot dream about Davis.

***

After several gulps of cold water and an even colder shower, I've finally pushed the dream about Davis somewhat out of my mind. I'm probably just excited about tonight. Though why I would dream about Davis like that instead of Jake is bothering me. I already know Davis is off limits. Maybe it's my subconscious just trying to get him out of my system. Hmmm. It's time to get ready to go out with Jake. I do my make-up and fix my hair in the only way it will go. It's straight. It never curls. Even as a kid when my mom would give me a perm, it just went back to being straight. Just as I am zipping up the back of my second open-toed bootie there is a light rap on the door.

"Hey, it's Jake. Biz? You ready?"

I open the door widely and put on my prettiest smile.

"Ta-Da."

Jake takes in my outfit. "Biz, you look great. You do know this is a college keg party, right?"

"What, too much?" I say, twirling slightly side to side.

"No, I just….No, you look great."

"Well, thank you Mr. Gianni," I tell him. I am ruthlessly flirting and batting my eyes. Honestly, I feel a little silly, but I am trying to demonstrate some confidence. I also might be feeling a little guilty for the Davis dream.

We drive to the party, which is in a part of town that is more eclectic than the suburb where Weldon is located. There are funky little shops, bars and restaurants, and musicians busking on the streets. The party is in an apartment in a brownstone. Jake tells me it is a musician friend that graduated last year who's throwing the party. Les or Wes or something like that. Entering, with Jake holding my hand, I notice there are a lot more guys than girls here. I hope Jake can't sense the shakiness I am feeling. I spot Charlie, Jules and Smitty over by a window looking out. Jake tells me he is going to get us a beer. I head over to my friends. We discuss the view from the apartment, how you can see all the way down to the Mississippi River and the city's unique skyline, that includes a certain famous Eero Saarinen monument. It's only a few minutes before Jake is back with a beer for both of us, in the ubiquitous red cups. The teasing begins, as Charlie and Smitty inform Jake what a terrible drinker I am. Terrible, because I cannot have more than two beers without becoming outrageously goofy. Jake seems intrigued, nodding his head with a smile.

"Yeah, I think this is probably it for me tonight," I inform him, raising my red cup.

Jake mumbles something I can't make out.

Seeing that a group of couches in the center of the large living room has just been vacated, Jules and I pull the boys over to sit down. Somehow the conversation turns and I realize the guys are playing the Who Would You Do? game. The game pretty much involves naming a person and discussing if you would "do" them and why or why not. I've played it before, but not since the beginning of junior year. Not since IT happened. Sitting between Jake and Jules, I do my best to act nonchalant about it. It's harmless, right?

Jules starts. "Would you do..." she draws out the question, "Smitty?" and turns to Charlie.

Charlie replies, "No," as do Jules, Jake and I. Smitty looks a little crushed, but then Suzette, who has approached our group, pipes in, "I'd consider it." Smitty perks up and pats the area between him and Jake for her to sit. She flounces prettily over to them and in a giggly voice says, "Hi, boys." They don't appear unhappy with the attention. Since Smitty was the last victim, it's his turn to ask.

"Would you do…Biz?"

I hide my face in my hands and lean forward, "Oh, no."

Jake puts his arm around me and begins pulling my hands away from my face.

"I'll answer that," he says to everyone. He turns and looks me in the eye and says, "Of course." Cheers and claps go up from my group of friends along with a few wolf whistles. I just smile and bite my lip.

Charlie says, "No," and winks at me. We both know why and share a visual acknowledgement. We have a history. Harmless, but still a history. Jules doesn't know. Jules doesn't notice our glances and I'm glad.

To the question of "doing" me, Jules says, "Yes."

"Thank you, girlfriend, right back at you."

Smitty dovetails onto the conversation, "I would like to say that I would, IF I could do Biz from the waist up and Jules from the waist down. That would be heaven."

Jules and I in unison screech, "Eeeewwww."

The group is laughing loudly now.

"Oh my God, Smitty, what a perv. Jesus, dude, are you drunk already?" Charlie scolds.

"Evidently…but seriously, think about it. That would be like the perfect chick." I am happy to hear no objections from the group. Jules and I thonk our plastic cups together in a toast to one another. I've already switched over to soda after about five sips of beer, since it looks like no one else is holding back and someone has to drive home.

Even though it's not her turn, Suzette interrupts the laughing and teasing with, "Would you do…Davis?" She directs it at Jules. *Shit. I am not answering that question. I've got to get away.* I reach over and place my hand on Jake's red cup.

"You want another?"

"That would be great, Bizzy," he answers with a satisfied smile. I see Smitty reach around Suzette to smack Jake on the arm and give him the up-nod and a smirk. I quickly make my escape to the next room to get Jake another beer.

Rounding the corner, I am stopped in my tracks by the sight of Davis. It's as if Suzette mentioning his name caused him to materialize here. I hadn't really thought of him since shaking off the dream, until she said his name. He's leaning against the archway near the keg, holding a beer. He has his eyes closed and his head down. I've never seen him out of his blacks… the black clothes he wears in the theatre and every time I've ever seen him. Except in the dream. Tonight he's wearing a red long sleeve Henley thermal shirt, low slung jeans, his usual black work boots and a very expensive looking watch. Hmm, I never noticed that before. The shirt clings to his upper body and I appreciate that he has the form of an upside down triangle. Broad, straight shoulders that taper down to his slim waist. The hum I feel whenever he's near vibrates low in by belly and moves lower. Aching almost. I swear it increases the closer I move toward him.

I approach and touch his arm, which only heightens the feeling down there, "Davis?"

He looks up and opens his stunning eyes at the same time to look at me. I can tell immediately he is already drunk.

"Lizzz-erd." he slurs. "Lizzz-erd Breath…you're here." With that he flings his arm over my shoulder and pulls me in for a squeeze.

"Let me pump you," he giggles at himself "…a beer."

I'm pretty sure I blush. "Um. That's okay, I'm just getting one for Jake."

"Oh, serving him are we? Nothing for you?"

"I'm good. I switched to Diet Coke. I'm the DD."

Looking down at my breasts, he teases with a growl, "You sure are."

It takes me a second to get his meaning, "Davis, I meant Designated Driver," I say, socking him on the bicep. He has no reaction to the punch. It sort of hurt my hand, his arm is so firm.

As he fills Jake's cup for me, he informs me, "Well, that's good because I am the Designated Drinker." He laughs again, gesturing to himself with the index finger of the hand that's holding his beer. Just so damn amused with himself. And I laugh too, admitting to myself, he is sort of a charming drinker.

Davis follows me back into the living room to the group and is met with sloppy drunken greetings from them all. A few more girls that I don't know have joined the group. Davis is the recipient of not a few kisses on the mouth and 'friendly' welcomes from the girls. Plenty of bro-hugs and up-nods are exchanged with the guys. He gives Suzette a hug and Jules an even bigger one along with a kiss on each cheek. *Where's my damn kiss?*

"Hey, missing your girl, Davis? Watch yourself, that one's mine. There's no shortage of babes here and you've never had any problem getting one before." Charlie laughs as he says it. I know he's not serious.

Davis moves away from Jules with a sort of jump, "Wazzn' thinking. Sorry, man. Just being friendly." He looks right at me, "Not looking for a babe." *Why is he looking at me when he says that?* I am confused by how I am drawn to and annoyed with Davis simultaneously.

Jules and Charlie both say to Davis, "It's okay" and look at each other with knowing smiles.

Thankfully, the Who Would You Do? game seems to be over. Suzette informs Davis that everyone present said they would "do" him.

"Everyone?" He asks looking around the group, but halts his gorgeous, slightly bloodshot eyes on me.

"Well, Biz went to get Jake's beer, so she didn't say, but the rest of the girls did…and Smitty." I think she is hitting on Davis. *Back off, Suzette.*

Smitty just nods and with an intoxicated grin yells across the room, "You are a boootiful man, Davis." Drunk. Great, now Smitty's hitting on him too.

I haven't had this much fun or laughed so much in a long, long time. Anytime I get up to get a beer for Jake, Davis follows and fills his own cup. He's at the point where he has to put his hand on my shoulder to make it to the keg. Jake has danced with me a few times, nuzzling his face into my neck. When he burps right on my neck while dancing, I decide it's time to go home. He agrees. Charlie has already left to take Jules home. She drank a lot. I'm sure she's already passed out in his bed. I ask Davis how he got there. He mumbles something about someone bringing him, but he thinks they left. After securing the keys to Jake's car, I drag the two intoxicated boys out of the apartment and pour them into the car. They both sing to me, loudly the whole way home. You haven't lived until you experience an alcohol-fueled serenade of Wake Me Up Before You, Go Go. I asked Davis repeatedly how to get to where he lives, but his directions don't make any sense. I'm tired and I don't want to drive around trying to figure it out, so I take him back to the Weldon. He can pass out there.

There is no way I am going to get these two idiots up to Jake's room by taking the stairs. After stumbling with an arm around each of their waists, into the front lobby, I squirm out from between them to punch the button to call the Disco elevator. They are laughing so hard they can't breathe and are leaning on one another for support. Jake whispers something into Davis' ear and looks at me.

"Really?" Davis questions, frowns a bit, then glances at me and chuckles. I am equal parts annoyed with them for getting so drunk and tickled by their joy. Together, they are a bit difficult to manage. All the way home and on the way in, either one or both of them are speaking to me with their faces WAY too close to mine. This must be what it smells like all the time when you work at a brewery.

I get help from both of them to open the elevator doors. I'm guessing it probably looks like a weird upright game of Twister is happening. I'm glad nobody is watching. We get in and each one leans on an opposite wall. I am standing in the middle, looking up, watching the numbers. When we get to the second floor, Jake walks out, then turns around, walks back in and kisses me soundly on the lips.

"Goodnight, Bizzy baby."

"Goodnight, Jake." It's not the ending to the evening I thought it would be. As he closes the door to the elevator, I say, "Hey, what about…" I was going to say 'Davis," but the door is practically shut.

I hear someone outside the elevator say, "Jake, hey Jake, need help to your room?"

The elevator proceeds up to my floor. Davis is still leaning against the carpeted wall, with his eyes closed. I think he is asleep. I'm pretty sure he missed dropping off Jake. Great, now what am I going to do with him?

As the elevator comes to a stop, Davis comes to life.

"Hey, Biz. Are you taking me home?"

"No, Davis. I think you have to sleep in my room."

"Alright," He doesn't say it in agreement. He says it as in an "alright, sounds good, sleeping with a girl" way. A hot, sexy way.

"No, Mavis, there is no 'Alright.' I'm tired. I am not one of your little playthings. You're drunk AND engaged, so you get to sleep on my floor."

"Party pooper." He is giggling like a teenage girl

"Absolutely. What's up with you tonight?"

He mumbles something like, "Not as much or many as you think," frowns, then goes silent.

Once in my dorm room, Davis immediately slides down to lie on the floor next to my bed. I lean against my bed and lift my leg behind me to take off my shoe. As I put that leg down and begin to lift the other, I feel Davis' hand running up and down the inside of my lower leg. It causes me to stop moving and tip my head back. It feels amazing. I inhale.

"Did you shave?" I don't make a move to push his hand away. He repeatedly slides it up to the inside of my knee and then slowly back down to cup it around my ankle. He rubs the bone of my ankle with his thumb. It feels incredible and the electrical hum and zap I feel every time I am around him magnifies. I just stand there and take it in. When I look down he is staring up at me. The stare is not sweet. Is it angry? No, it's hot. Scorching.

"Uh huh." I say breathlessly, taking a moment to clear my head before I respond to the question.

His hand stops moving, but stays on the inner part of my upper knee. I swear there are flames shooting up to the space between my legs. If he goes any higher he'll feel my excitement.

69

"Did you do it for Jake?"

I don't know what comes over me, but I'm suddenly pissed off. So what if I did it for Jake? What's it to Davis? And why did he have to ruin the amazing feeling by insinuating that I was planning to sleep with Jake?

Moving away toward the bathroom and away from his touch, which I instantly miss, I throw back at him, "I shave every few days. I don't do it for anyone but me." I think I hear him whisper, "Too bad."

After changing into my lounge pants and tank top, I grab an extra pillow and blanket from my bed and throw them at the now half-dressed man on my floor. His shirt and belt are in a pile next to the door. His chest and arms are surprisingly toned. I realize I've only ever seen his forearms unclothed before. *Wow, I could look at that chest all night.* There is a small tattoo on his upper chest on the side I can't see. I wonder what it says? His eyes follow my every move, causing me to quickly avert mine. I climb into my bed and then hang my face and one arm over. Davis is arranging himself with the pillow and blanket. It is not unpleasant to watch at all. I push a pillow between my knees.

"Just go to sleep, Mavis. Oh, and if you are going to puke, don't do it on my floor. Crawl over to the bathroom. I left the toilet seat up."

"First time a girl's ever been cool with that." His comment makes me grin. Smiling his scorching, smirky smile, he reaches his hand up to me. I reach my hand down and can just barely touch his fingertips. Wouldn't you know it, even in that brief touch there is a charge of connection. The electricity shoots right up my arm to my chest.

"Night, Davis."

His arm falls back over his head. "What's your deal, Lizard Breath? How come you go from hot to cold, shy to smart ass all the time? Figuring you out is making me crazy." It's a legitimate question. I have to give him that.

I flip to my back, sighing and staring at the ceiling, "Don't try, sweetie, I think I'm screwed up."

"Sweetie" he repeats my term of endearment. "Me, too."

Me, too? Like he agrees I'm screwed up or is he saying he is screwed up? I lean back over the side of the bed and look down at Davis. He's rolled over onto his stomach, so I can't see his hard, beautiful chest anymore. Although his back is pretty gorgeous to gaze at, too. His face is turned toward me. He's sound asleep with a small sad smile on his lips. I'd like to watch him all night.

***

I wake to sun streaming in through the sides of my blinds. Not a clue what time it is, I roll over to see how my overnight guest is doing from a hangover perspective.

He's not there. I didn't dream last night, too, did I? As I begin to sit up in bed, I hear a key in the lock of my door. Oh my god, who's there? Did I leave my key in the lock last night? I've done that before. I was a bit preoccupied. I sit upright and pull the covers up, even though I am wearing a tank top and lounge pants. A disgustingly chipper, fully dressed Davis comes through the door and throws my keys on the desk.

"Mornin' Lizard Breath." He has two large cups of coffee.

"Did you steal my keys?"

"I wouldn't call it stealing, since I came back. You were asleep. Snoring like a baby hamster." He does his imitation of a baby hamster snoring. Cute. "I couldn't bear to wake you."

Seeing that he's brought coffee, I tell him, "I guess I forgive you."

"I don't know what came over me last night. I hardly ever get drunk."

I tilt my head and shrug. "It wasn't quite the evening I had anticipated, but it was fun."

"You thought you'd be spending it primarily with Jake, huh? Not babysitting a couple of drunks." He sounds down. "How is Jake?"

"I'm sure he's fine. I haven't checked on him yet." I think I catch Davis grin.

"He doesn't know about this?" Davis is gesturing with his finger to the two of us and then around the room to the floor and bed.

"No, I don't think he needs to know. Since, really it was nothing and you passed out."

His upbeat expression fades when I say the word " nothing."

"Yeah, sorry about that." Davis FINALLY hands me a cup of coffee. "Please accept this with my apologies." He teases and bows to me as if I'm royalty. I inhale and take a sip. It's perfect. He fixed it just the way I like it. How did he know? I make a little noise of

appreciation. Davis looks pleased.

I let him off the hook with "THIS is definitely a start, " as I lift

my coffee cup in salute.

We both pause and look at each other. I can feel tension building

between us and then Davis seems to shake a thought off and

completely changes courses.

"Hey, Lizard. I gotta go. But before I do…" He takes my

iPod out of his pocket and moves toward me. I am still sitting in my

elevated bed. Cupping my face, he runs both hand up my jawline and

puts the ear buds in my ears. He gently kisses my forehead.

"I am really sorry, Sweetie." He winks. He's repeating my

term of endearment from last night. "Turn that on after I leave."

Before he walks out the door, he turns, winks again, and says, "Have

Fun."

I prop myself back on the pillows and take a sip of my perfect

coffee. Turning on the iPod, I hear and see the song he's cued up—

Sorry by Buckcherry. Oh, man. I think I'm in trouble.

***

I loll around in bed for another hour or so, chewing over last night and listening to more songs. I get up and stretch and take a quick shower. Not washing my hair, just plopping on my favorite black cadet cap, I leave my room and walk down the stairs to the second floor to check on Jake.

I knock softly on his door. There is a thump from inside like someone falling out of bed. The door opens slightly. A portion of Jake's face appears. He looks rough. His hair is totally jacked up. I must have woken him. He only opens the door a crack.

"Hi" I whisper gently in case his head hurts.

"Uh" is his only response.

"You hungover?" I ask.

"Yes. I think I might still be a little drunk." He looks really bad and uncomfortable.

"Okay, I'll talk to you later. Text or call me if you need anything."

"I think I just need to go back to bed. Bye."

It's weird, Davis seemed so much more drunk than Jake last night, but Jake's the one unable to get out of bed the next day.

Chapter 7: NOW-October into November

The semester is really amping up now. Days are filled with classes, work at The Space getting ready for Othello, and once a week dinners with Charlie and Jake at China Garden. It is kind of a new tradition started a few weeks ago. They came by my room and asked me to go out to eat with them and it just caught on. Another new activity I've started attending is Game Night in the Turrets. Lawrence Dorm has these two turrets on the end. From outside they make the building look like a castle. Inside, the turret feature results in two round rooms at the end of each hall. They weren't practical for dorm rooms I guess, so they became lounge areas. The second floor, where Jake and Suzette live, started Game Nights. These nights are now advertised around the dorms on flyers. They consist of residents bringing their board games and snacks to the turrets and setting up tables to play. Anyone can join. It's a fun, inexpensive night, perfect for college students. It's amazing how competitive some of the residents get about Mah-Jong. Mah-Jong. My grandma plays that game. Sometimes there are even Game Afternoons on Sundays.

I am at The Space a lot. Jake is rehearsing a lot. The only time we seem to see each other is at lunch or if I stop by after work. I'll text him on my walk back to the dorm. If he's home he generally tells me to stop by. I don't stay too long since it's usually late. My visits consist of listening to music, which Jake is very knowledgeable about, having a drink and making out. I am learning more and more about Jazz and Classic Rock. And the making out is pretty hot. It's lots of kissing and mashing, but never gets too intense. If it ever does or Jake's hands start straying into places I'm uncomfortable with, I stop it and say I have to get up early. Jake never complains. It's so nice to not feel overwhelmed with the need to please or cave. He is always sweet to me when I leave. He could be just the guy I need.

Time spent at The Space is non-stop activity. One day, near the end of October, I'm heading into work when I spot Davis heading to his big, black SUV. Its new, fancy. The passenger compartment windows are blacked out. A Cadillac, I think. Much nicer than most college students have. When he sees me he turns and I see under his black leather jacket he is wearing a white t-shirt that says in black letters, "It's All Fun and Games Until Someone Posts the Video." I shake my head and laugh tightly. It IS a funny shirt, but something about it makes me uneasy.

"Nice shirt." I manage to chirp out in an attempt to remain cool.

"It's true."

"Stop," I say trying to push down the uneasy feeling, but remain joking. I put my hand up and wave it back and forth frantically. "I don't want to know any more." That makes him laugh.

"What's with the Escalade?" I ask, changing the subject to his car.

Davis looks down and stares at his feet. He kicks something on the ground before answering. "Uh…I need something I can haul things in. I would have preferred a truck, but my mother has become a bit of a safety freak. I think she would have been happiest if I drove a tank," Davis laughs. "So the Escalade is a concession. My dad scored it from a connection. From a looks perspective, it makes my mom happy in a superficial way, too." The way he talked about his dad having a connection and the blacked out SUV, I joke to Davis that it sounds like his dad is in the Mafia.

Davis' only response is, "Nothing like that, Lizard," before he drops the subject.

Davis tells me he's going to the lighting supply store and invites me to go with him. I am the only one manning the costume shop tonight, so I pause for a beat. When he says we'll be back in thirty minutes, I throw my bag in the front seat and hop in. We haven't gone very far when Davis' cell rings.

"Hi, Babe. How are you doing?" A girl? One of his many? Or his fiancée? "On my way to pick up some lighting instruments with Biz." He's told her about me? "Yes, I am. I told you I would be there. I've got it all planned out. I miss you, too. Okay, Babe. I'll call you later when we can talk more. Mmmhmm, you too" He's very sweet with her. I wonder how he can be like that and also be the player I've heard he is. I feel moderately uncomfortable listening to their conversation. And a bit jealous.

The lighting supply store has Davis' order ready when we arrive. I don't even get out of the car. Davis runs in and comes out with two lights. We are back to The Space in well under thirty minutes. As I head to the costume shop I tell Davis, "Even though you ARE a total player, you seem like a very good fiancée. That was her, right?"

"Yes." He sounds slightly annoyed because his "Yes" comes off like an "Of course."

"She's very lucky. What's her name?" I ask.

"Kathleen."

"I hope she knows how lucky she is to have you."

"Even though, I'm a playah? " He teases sarcastically. "She's a good girl. She's been with me through some bad times. I think she is having a difficult time with me being so far away. I won't see her until Thanksgiving when I go to visit my Mom and Dad."

Davis heads into The Space to give the lights to the crew. I go to check with the actors to see if there are any rehearsal costume pieces they need or have misplaced.

I finally get to the costume shop to find a gorgeous, bare-chested Davis changing, pulling his black jeans over a pair of Stewie

Griffin boxers. His sense of humor constantly surprises me. And his semi-undressed state has pushed thoughts of his fiancée right out of my head. I'm pretty sure my jaw drops at his hotness.

"You have Stewie boxers?"

"Yes, Yes, I do" He says in a Stewie voice. "I think they are smashing."

He continues to use the cartoon voice and tease me by calling me by all my different names, like Stewie does to Lois on Family Guy. "Biz, Elizabeth, Bizzy, Lizard Breath..." until just like Lois, I say, "WHAT?" He is obviously pleased I know the joke. He nudges me and says, "Hi," like Stewie would. Then gives me a big hug. His arms sweep around my waist and while he pulls me in, I take in a big inhalation of the clean, manly Davis smell. He strokes his thumbs up and down my lower back. He begins to back away slightly from the embrace and look down at me. I shift my gaze rapidly between his eyes and lips.

"What's up in here?" Jules has appeared in the doorway. I back away from Davis and out of his arms. She is taking in the view that is Davis' chest.

"Oh, we were just messing around," I evade. I'm trying to appear cool and not like I'm having the time of my life joking around and being swept up by this sexy, funny guy.

Davis slips on his black thermal. Right before he does, I finally get a look at the tattoo on his upper left chest. In beautiful script that connects in one stroke, I read the name, COLE.

He says hi and bye to Jules, "See ya, Jules....." and then, stepping closer, lifting my chin with his index finger and gazing deeply into my eyes with his hypnotizing green ones, adds "Lizard... Have Fun," in the Stewie voice. Chuckling, he leaves us without looking back. We both watch him walk out. I'm sure Jules is checking out his ass. I know I am.

Jules waits until she knows Davis has left the room to turn on me, "Biz, he is into you. So into you."

"No he's not, he's just goofing off with me like a brother or a friend."

"Uh, that is not brotherly or friendly. Did you not pay attention when your Mom told you that boys tease you because they like you?"

"Boys, Jules, Boys."

"Admit it, you like him." Jules cajoles.

"He's a known player, Jules!"

She counters with, "It's strange. I don't see as many girls hanging around Davis as there were this summer. It looks like he stopping fooling around."

"Whatever. I just heard him talking to his fiancée. He seemed really sincere. Maybe he's changed. Maybe he's settling down. If you must know, yes, I like him, but even if he's not a player, he is ENGAGED. The most we could ever be is friends. "

"That is seriously too bad. You guys are funny together. He doesn't look like he's thinking about his fiancée when he's talking to you. You'd make a very hot couple."

"We're friends. I'm with Jake."

"How's that going?"

I describe to her how Jake is so even, after the roller coaster ride known as Neil. Jake is definitely good looking. He has a unique and sexy "old school jazz" way of dressing-fedoras, suit jackets. More than that, he's intellectually accessible. Neil always made me feel inferior in that regard, talking about Kierkegaard and Buber all the time. He could fucking rationalize any and all of his selfish behavior by quoting some philosopher or theory or belief, as long as it served his purpose. At the time, I thought he was brilliant. Now, I'm beginning to suspect he was a sociopath. Utterly blameless in his own eyes for every hurtful thing he did to anyone. Including that woman who was carrying his child. In the end, he destroyed my self-confidence and left me with little to laugh or find joy about in my life.

Jake is patient. Our moments of mild sexual contact are slowly heating up at a pace I can control. We are close to moving toward the next level. Jake was......

Not Davis.

I like Jake. I am totally at ease around him, until the physical aspect gets too intense. He doesn't make me laugh and annoyingly, I don't come alive like I do around Davis, but he's sweet. The electricity, the buzz I feel whenever Davis looks at me or was in any sort of proximity to me is not there with Jake. It unnerves me and excites me simultaneously. Emotional lines are getting blurry. I know I like Jake, but I'm attracted in every way to Davis. Davis is not mine to be attracted to.

***

As rehearsal is wraps up for the evening, Kris, who is stage managing the show, calls me into The Space on the PA system. She

84

tells me PJ needs my assistance and to bring my sewing kit. When I get there Kris directs me to the actor playing Iago. He is on the stage, standing off to one side talking to PJ. PJ flounces up to me, puts his arm around my waist and directs me to the actor. With a loud, "Girlfriend, help me!" he tells me that Iago has broken a fastener on his breeches. The other actors are milling around, having just been given their notes. Kris tells them to go change out of the costume pieces they were trialing in the partial dress rehearsal. I kneel in front of the actor and examine the fastener that is no longer holding his breeches up. It's in front and a little off to the side. The lights on the stage are changing to sultry and moody dark pinks and reds. It's not uncommon for the light crew to experiment with the lighting after a rehearsal, so I ignore it and go about my task. I can hear the crew and Davis in the booth. I realize I've forgotten my scissors, so after I reinforce the fastener, I can't cut the thread. Not thinking, I lean forward and bite the string with my teeth. It doesn't come loose. At some point during this, the lighting has become even more "Strip Club" and the kind of "Bow chicka wow wow" music that can be heard in a porn film starts blaring in The Space. As I go in to bite the thread again, I hear riotous laughter. PJ is bent over with both his

85

hands on his knees, practically crying. One of the laughs is Davis'.

Oh My GOD. I realize what I am doing looks like I am giving the

actor playing Iago a blow job. I freeze. Then in several quick moves,

I look up at PJ and then the booth, grab my sewing supplies and run

from The Space.

Still cackling, PJ yells after me, "Bizzy, Girlfriend...don't be

mad. It was a joke, sweetie."

I hear Davis say loudly, "Oh, Shit." And then reprimand

everyone, "God Dammit, Guys!"

Chapter 8: NOW, about THEN

There is a scuffle going on in the hall outside the costume shop. All I can make out is PJ's voice and then Davis'. Finally, I catch what's going on. "I've got it, PJ...I mean Phillip. No, really you've done enough. We've all done enough. I'll check on her. Just get the actors out of their costumes for her. Please?"

PJ tells Davis, "Sure, sure...just tell her I'm sorry. I didn't think she'd react that way."

Davis finds me in the shop putting my supplies away. I sniffle and stiffen my posture. I don't want to look at him. That little episode onstage is just the sort of interaction I am trying to avoid. I am using all the skills I learned this summer to keep it together.

"Lizard, are you okay? They were just fooling around. They didn't mean anything." I can't look at him. "What's wrong." He comes up behind me.

I hesitate and then it all crashes out of me in a tsunami of words and emotions. "Davis, the last day of spring semester last year something…happened." I start to cry as he steps in front of me. I just cannot bring myself to look at him. The only thing holding me together is my mantra and the knowledge that soon this moment will be over. If I look at him I will crack.

"What, what happened, Lizard Breath?" He is holding one of my arms at the elbow and with his other hand stroking my hair behind my ear to try and see my face. Lizard Breath. Even crying, the name makes me smile a bit. In a deluge of words and tears, I tell him how Neil used me roughly and left suddenly the night before school was out. Davis' grip on my arm becomes tight and his eyebrows pull together.

I continue, "I went back to my room and cried myself to sleep. I didn't hear from him. The next morning I had to help residents with the final clean out and inspections of their rooms. I don't know how I got through that." I take a deep breath and continue with the story.

"After the last resident was out, I gathered my backpack, locked my room and went to Little Jan's office. We had a serious discussion about me coming back as an RA the next year. She'd decided to give me another chance. I probably looked exhausted and contrite after all the crying I'd done the night before. I was exhausted, even though the crying wasn't about the miserable way I had failed at my job.

I decided to have lunch before I went to my new place down the street. I'd call Neil from there, I decided. I already had a feeling of dread when I entered the cafeteria. Stepping through the doors to the cafeteria, I saw Jules being yelled at by a tall woman in her mid to late twenties with wavy brown hair back in a ponytail, red faced and visibly pregnant.

"Where is the little SLUT?" the unknown woman bellowed.

As I sprinted up to help my friend I saw NEIL was right next to this woman.

"What's going on, Neil? Jules? Who's this?"

The woman turned on me, "Are you Biz?"

I responded, "Yes"

She straightened, took a step toward me and said, "Stay the FUCK AWAY from Neil. You got me?" My mouth fell open, but

89

nothing came out. I looked at Neil. He stepped up next to the woman, put his arm around her and announced, proudly:

"This is Robyn, my fiancée. We broke up in December, but we are back together now…and we're pregnant."

Heaving sobs, I could only get out "What about us? What about last night?"

Neil snorted loudly, "There is no 'us.' And last night. . .you know exactly what last night was." He and Robyn both smirked. Dazed, I was about to collapse, but Jules and Charlie were at my side and lowered me into a chair, as they screamed Neil and Robyn out of the cafeteria.

I knew what last night was. A humiliating good-bye fuck for his dirty little piece on the side.

As I finish telling the story to Davis, I realize I am crying almost as hard as I was on that day. Davis holds me close to his chest and slowly we back toward a theatre seat stored in the shop. He sits down, holding me and seating me on his lap at the same time. He doesn't say a word, but his arms are a bit tense and his back sort of straight. He slowly strokes my arm while I sigh repeatedly to stop the crying. When I can eventually look up, Davis strokes my hair away from my face, pushing it behind my ears. He pulls a red bandana out of his back pocket and gently wipes the streaks of tears off my face. Contritely, he tells me, "I'm sorry the guys' teasing brought this all up."

"Davis, it's always right here," I point to my head and then my heart. "I work so hard to keep the memories from haunting me, but I am always a word or an action away from falling apart."

He speaks slowly and deliberately. His voice is low, like he's trying to maintain control. His lips barely moving, "I am so sorry, Biz. I can't believe anyone could do that to you. It makes me incredibly angry." *That's what his tension is about.* "Are they around anymore?" I tell him I haven't seen them since that day, but they live in town. I dread running into them. I ask Davis to never tell anyone what I've told him. I don't think I have to, but I do anyway. Enough people know. The cafeteria wasn't very busy on that last day of school, but word gets out. Davis stands me up, takes my hand, pulls me in for a long comforting hug and kisses the top of my head. The feeling of relief and safety I have in my friend's arms is enough to make me cry again, but I don't.

I've never seen angry Davis before. I can feel the rage flying off him when he tells me, "Fuckers. God help either one of them if I ever run into them."

"That isn't all."

Really-pissed-off Davis emerges. "What? They did more?"

"Not them…me." Davis looks very confused.

So I explain it to Davis. All of it. The episode in the cafeteria was horrible, but it's what I did after that, what none of my friends or family knew about, what happened after I grabbed my backpack and while sobbing heavily, left campus and walked down the street three blocks.

Chapter 9: THEN-Last Summer

I'm unsure how I was even able to do it, but after a few moments, I stood, gathered my backpack, and without a word, on shaky legs left the cafeteria. I made my way down the street to Neil's friend, Randall's house in a fog of tears and heaving sobs. Once there, I put the key that I was given a few days ago in the lock and went in. Randall is not there. I trudged up the stairs to my new room, threw my backpack on the bed, kicked off my shoes and curled up on the bed and continued to cry softly. I heard my phone blowing up with voice mails and texts. After a few minutes I took it out, turned it off and dropped it off the side of the bed. I stayed in that position for three days. I only got up to pee. That's it. Right back to bed. No shower.

No eating. No drinking. Cry, sleep, pee, sleep, cry, cry, cry, pee, sleep. It was only after getting up to pee sometime during that third day that I felt faint and had to sit back down on the bed. My head was throbbing. I managed to get to the bathroom. I quickly drank a large glass of water and just as quickly threw it all up into the toilet. I didn't want to be there. I wanted to disappear. Some sort of survival instinct must have kicked in because I eventually drank a bit more water and kept it down. Then I headed downstairs and made a bowl of cereal. Randall appeared and told me I looked like crap. Nice. He stood too close. Evidently, he had no sense of a person's personal bubble. Smelled like cigarettes and old liquor. I'd only met him a couple of times with Neil. Randall isn't a bad looking guy, he has similar coloring to Neil. He has a scrawny, yet muscular build, a few days' beard growth, unwashed hair. A shower wouldn't hurt. Randall appears to be stuck in the "grunge era." He seems old to be one of Neil's friends, but I figured if Neil trusted him, it would be cool to live there. I felt less sure now. Moving away from him to regain a little of my own space, I looked at the girlie calendar on the wall of the kitchen and realized I had to report to work at the theatre tomorrow. I didn't want to leave the house. Someone that knows me, who saw what

94

happened, might see me. Randall told me I owed him $500 for the first month's rent. That decided it for me-I had to go to work tomorrow or call my parents to come get me and take me home. I couldn't let them see me like this. After the cereal, I felt a little better. I took two pain relievers and downed a glass of whiskey from Randall's liquor cabinet. Randall watched all this with a creepy interest. I realized I needed to remember to act less vulnerable around him. I said goodnight and returned to my sad bed in my sad room.

***

The days ran together and went something like this: Get up at 3:00 in the afternoon, eat ramen or soup or a peanut butter and jelly sandwich, go to work as an usher, go to the Alumni House or whatever party is around, get drunk, sometimes bring home a random guy, let him screw me. Repeat. In ten days, I had sex with at least as many nameless guys. Oh, wait, one guy I actually banged twice. I think his name was Mick. I thought, "Who the fuck cares? I am just what Neil's woman, Robyn said, a slut." I thought the mindless hooking up would make me feel better, and while it was happening, it did, briefly. It didn't last and in the morning, I felt crappy about myself again. That didn't stop me from getting rip roaring drunk and doing it the next night. So the pattern changed. Sleep, work, drink, drink, drink, fuck, sleep, sleep, drink, fuck.

About two weeks into all of this, after a particularly drunken night, Randall came to my room and demanded his $500 for my part of the rent. I didn't have it. I used any money I'd earned to drink. He pulled my cup full of whatever I was drinking out of my hand, took a swig and threatened me that either I "get with" him, every night for the rest of the month, or get out. I was horrified and felt trapped. I told him I'd get him the money and to "get the fuck out." He handed the cup back to me, sloshing some of the contents over the rim. Crying and looking in the mirror after his ultimatum, I knew what I had to do. Resolved, I downed what was left in the cup. I needed to make the call to my father to come get me. And I did, right before I passed out.

Telling Davis this part of the story, the part nobody knows except me, the men I screwed and my counselor, I am mortified. Horrified at myself. I haven't even told him about the next morning, when I found myself on top of my bed completely naked after passing out. I can't remember what happened. My counselor and I tried to uncover it during my sessions this past summer. I have no memory of the rest of the night after calling my Dad. I have a feeling deep in my subconscious that I do know and just can't let myself admit it. While telling all of this to Davis, I purposely omit that part and how I recovered over the summer. I wouldn't be surprised if he shoved me away and stormed off, if I did reveal it. I wouldn't be surprised if he never talked to me again. Skank. It's what I would do if I were him. I'd run away. Fast. Run away from the damaged chick, but he doesn't. Davis holds me and rocks me.

"Davis, I think I killed my soul." I wail and grasp at him with my chin over his shoulder as he continues to hold me tight. "I can't remember me...Biz...before Neil. Before I let all those guys.... I remember I was happy. Not a care in the world. Fun. Not scared of anything."

"Oh, baby" Davis whispers and tries to shush my crying.

"I am scared all the time. Of everything. I have to remind myself every moment to keep going. To not be scared. To get out. Be with people. Interact. I have been forcing myself to act like a human since I got back to school. I have been talking myself into dating. Into...being with Jake." Davis' arms tense around me. I am gasping for little breaths while sobbing out my story. "The only time I feel like me is when I am talking to you." I sense Davis' arms relaxing.

Sighing, Davis pulls me back to look at my puffy tear-stained face. He gives me a small smile. "Lizard, baby, your soul isn't dead. Your heart is broken. You aren't the only one that has ever been crushed. Not the only one that has made a bad choice in the face of humiliation. It's a way to try and push the pain away." He is speaking sincerely, like he's had this kind of experience. *What kind of pain has Davis had to endure?*

"Neil and that woman?" His voice is seething hatred. "Those guys? They thought nothing of destroying you for their own fun. They preyed on your sweetness and trusting nature. You're lucky you got away from that Randall guy." That statement makes me catch my breath briefly, but Davis doesn't seem to notice. He just pulls me to him again and strokes my hair to comfort me. It is incredibly soothing and thrilling simultaneously. I won't deny it, it's getting me a little worked up.

"Your heart – it's broken because you were hurt. Not because of anything you did or how much you drank or who you had sex with. You were hurt. They hurt you. Baby, it's not your fault."

98

"My mother always told me I was too trusting as a kid." I explain to him. "If someone took a toy or a snack from me, I would just stand there and cry, not understanding why anyone would hurt me. I guess I never learned. I always want to trust."

"You know the people who really know you — Jules, Charlie – they really care about you. They don't want to destroy you or take advantage of you. They'd never do anything that would hurt you at all. They want to build you up. They...WE have been trying since September. We know you. We want all of you back."

Wait. Davis said, "We."

"You care?"

Davis laughs gently. He tells me slowly, "Whether you like it or not, I care about you. I'm yours. Uh..your friend. Are you so blind? Come on, would I call you Lizard Breath if I didn't care?" He shoots me one of his smirky smiles.

He's mine? Right, my "friend." So not really MINE.

I wipe tears off my cheeks, feeling a bit of a smile starting on my lips. "So that's not you being a smart ass...that's you being affectionate?"

"I know it's weird, little Lizard baby. It's just how I am. How I work. I, unlike you, am not a wordy person."

"I'm wordy?"

"Have you heard you?" He is smiling and grinning at me. It makes me feel lighter. I smile back through my fading sniffles.

"I get excited. You know the rapid talking thing? It's nerves. I used to be a supreme smart ass. All about the fun. Your favorite slogan: 'Have Fun!' could have been MY saying. Everything was light, humorous, all about the fun. I sang all the time. Laughed a lot. Everything became a crazy adventure and everyone had a snarky nickname connected to them."

"See," Davis says to get me to pause, "Wordy. You haven't lost it, if you still do all those things. Nobody has EVER attempted to call me Mavis before."

Under my breath I say, "You mean to your face." He laughs so I guess it was just loud enough for him to hear. "I'm sure people called you that all the time and you didn't realize it. It's just too easy. Davis, seriously, it's just a short walk to Mavis."

"You're still a supreme smart ass."

I am laughing, really laughing and being held. By my friend. I never would have thought telling anyone about my horrible shame could end like this.

We are both quiet for a while. Davis runs his hand over my hair and clears his throat, before speaking, "I want you to consider doing something, Biz. Just think about it and see what might happen." He has gotten a little bit more serious, but I can tell he is trying to keep it light. "What would happen if you walked away from situations or people instead of trying to hold on to them, keep them happy. You try so hard to appear to have it together and make sure everyone is happy, and in the end you make yourself unhappy. What would happen if you asked for what YOU wanted instead of just willingly taking what's given you? Would you fall apart if someone said, "No?"

"I never saw it that way before," I answer honestly. Part of me wants to get defensive and be pissed about what he is saying. He makes me sound like such a sucker. The other part, the part that is exhausted, just listens and tries to get it.

"In our life, there are the ones that go away and the ones that stay. People, things, situations. Which ones are the ones worth working on, fighting for? You need to ask for what you want."

And he called me the Wordy one.

Chapter 10: NOW-Halloween

Boxwood has gained a mini following in the weeks since school started. They have been playing small gigs down on the Loop as they perfect their sound. Now, the guys have scored big, though. They have been asked to play the Weldon Halloween Bash. It's a notorious blow out held every Halloween and sponsored by Bored Board. There is no Greek System at Weldon to hold parties. Bored Board is just what the name implies. A board of people that plans events to keep everyone from getting bored. Halloween is Bored Board's premiere fall event. In second semester it's Springfest, a giant outdoor party.

The Halloween party is being thrown in the Alumni House, also known as The Lum. It's the only place on campus where liquor can be served. Supposedly, you can only drink if you are 21 and have a wristband. That's the theory, anyway.

Besides Boxwood playing, there is a DJ for breaks. Charlie, Jake, Simon and Colin went over early to set up and sound check. Jules went with Charlie, of course. Davis told me he is running their lights and sound, so I'm sure he's there, too. The Lum is only a short walk from the dorms, but Smitty is going to come by and walk with me there. When he arrives, I survey his costume. Either he is dressed like a nerdy drag queen or Garth from the Wayne's World movies. Long blonde wig, black framed glasses and a fancy camera around his neck.

Finally, it hits me, "Oh...I get it... Annie Leibovitz." Of course, what would a photographer go as but another photographer. I am dressed as a bunny. Not a sexy bunny. Just a bunny. I have on a white velour track suit and I've made ears out of a pair of white tube socks and coat hangers. I've sewn them to the hood of my jacket. On my feet are a pair of very fluffy white sheep skin slippers I've borrowed from Suzette, authentic Uggs, a gift from her parents when they went to Australia.

We talk and joke on the walk to The Lum. When we arrive the party is already pumping. Boxwood is on a makeshift stage on one end of the large main room. I smile and wave to all of them and blow a kiss to Jake. He takes a hand off his guitar to catch it. So cute. I indicate that I am going to get a beer from the kitchen and will be right back. It might be the relief of sharing my secret shame with Davis and getting it off my mind or just the celebration in general, but I decide to drink tonight. I don't have to drive so I might as well go for it.

Beer in hand, I wander around the party. One of the best things about this school is the level of talent and creativity. The Halloween costumes are outrageous. I can't decide my favorite. The couple dressed as voodoo dolls – anatomically correct voodoo dolls with giant stick pins included; the guy dressed as Slash; or Buddy the Elf. Everyone seems to be really enjoying themselves and letting loose. I down my first beer like it's water. Heading back to the keg for a second, I run into Jules. She is dressed as a 60's go-go girl. Mini dress, go-go boots, silver wig. She could not be more adorable. She matches Charlie, who's channeling Mick Jagger a la 1969. When I look more closely it appears that the guys in Boxwood are all dressed like famous musicians from different eras. Jake is Eddie Van Halen. He looks so different with dark hair. Simon has on nothing but his whitey-tighies. Guess he's Flea from Red Hot Chili Peppers. Colin, recently recruited as the permanent drummer, has on a pair of ear phones duct taped to his head. Aaahhh, Keith Moon.

"Hey," Jules shouts over the music, "Are you drinking tonight?"

"Yes, yes I am."

"Hurray, Party Biz! I like your costume."

Ever the wise ass, I tell her, "I'm a bunny."

"Duh!"

Beer number two leads to numbers three and four. I am having a great time. Dancing with Jules and then Smitty for many songs. Standing in front of the band and singing at the top of my lungs. I haven't cut loose in so long. It feels freeing. I remember that Davis is supposed to be working the sound. I look around the large room and spot him in the back. He is all in black and wearing earphones, too. No duct tape. No costume. His eyes are already on me as I find him and move toward him. He motions for me to come over to the sound board by him. He watches me the entire time I walk toward him. Hugging me with one arm when I get to him, he kisses my head through my hood. The vibration, the spark, the zapping buzzing electricity never lessens, only gets stronger and more intense when I'm with him. You'd think it would go away but it doesn't. I have gotten so I look forward to it. Crave it.

Davis takes my red cup full of beer and puts it behind him on the table, telling me it wouldn't be good to spill it on the equipment. I frown as he takes it from me, but stop as he pulls me into his arms for a bigger hug.

"Hey, little Lizard Bunny."

I correct him, "I am Alcohol Bunny! Drink up!"

Davis chuckles at me, "Wow, you are really enjoying yourself, aren't you?"

"Yes, because I am NOT the DD." He smirks at me and nods his head, as I add, "And I need to PAARRRR-TEEE."

I dance with Davis for a few songs behind the sound board. Occassionally I step away from the board to drink a bit more, but come right back to be with Davis. Boxwood has announced that they are taking a break. Jake comes to the sound board, greets Davis, and

107

wrapping an arm around me, gives me a kiss square on the mouth. I am about to take it up a notch, when Jake pulls away and asks, "Bizzy, are you....drunk?"

"Maybe."

Davis nudges me and pipes in, raising one of his eyebrows at Jake, "She's Alcohol Bunny."

"I'm Alcohol Bunny."

"Lucky me," Jake says under his breath, sarcastically. Davis' eyebrows have pinched together. "I think I'll go get a drink," Jake informs me.

"Good idea, Jakey." I slur and then shout, holding my beer up, "Drink up!" Davis is smiling to himself and shaking his head.

Jake tells me he'll see me in a bit. The DJ has taken over and is playing a slow song. I dance with Davis, melting into him. He feels SOOOO nice. I nuzzle his chest a little. Davis sighs. *Whoa, Biz.* Where the hell is Jake? He hasn't come back. I pull back from Davis' arms.

"I'm going to go look for Jake."

Davis protests, but eventually allows me to leave. I grab my cup and head for the kitchen. No Jake. I wander all over the house and cannot find him. There is a small salon on the other side of the house that is less full and quieter. I decide to sit there for a while.

Looking up from…wherever it is I am lying, I see Davis leaning over me. When did I lie down? He is moving me to sit up. I shoot him a smile. He is so FUCKING HANDSOME. I wonder if I said that out loud? I just sit and stare at him. Both of him. They both shoot their panty-scorching smirky smile at me. *Whoa! Two Davis'.* I think I'm drunk. *Focus. Now there is only one. Still Hot.* He is kneeling in front of me, holding both my arms near the shoulders and scanning my face. He has taken off his black hoodie. The t-shirt he is wearing has one word on it, TRICK.

I point at his shirt, "TRICK, cute."

"See? Not wordy." He points at himself and the word on his shirt.

Leaning forward, I move my face close and put my forehead right against his. Throwing my arms over his shoulders I tell him, "I think YOU are the trick, Davis. One big trick on me…So where's the TREA…T?" Mmm. Sliding my face down his cheek, I rest my head on my arm by his face and turn to admire him. Gorgeous face. I feel his hard muscled upper back with my hands. Whoa. Sleepy. He smells so yummy.

***

Where am I? Oh, I'm in my room. I'm sitting on the floor. I hear loud talking outside my room.

I hear Davis' voice. He sounds angry. "NO. You are not! She's…"

I fall back on the hardwood floor, OW and, look, there's the ceiling…

***

I awake facing a wall. I think it's the wall next to my bed. I hope it's the wall next to my bed. I see that yes, it is, and I sigh with relief. My head is pounding. I swear I can hear the sunlight bouncing off the wall. Even light is too loud. I smack my lips. Yuck, cotton mouth. I reach back to turn over and feel… ohmigod. Shit, shit, shit. Someone is here in bed with me. I am sweaty and some of my hair is sticking to the side of my face. I haven't even lifted my head and I am paralyzed with fear. What did I do last night? I look under the sheet and light blanket that are over me. I am wearing a black tank top and pink boy shorts. My bra is still on. That's a good sign, right? I close

110

my eyes and roll over. I don't know what I'm hoping to see when I open my eyes. Jules, I'm hoping it's Jules, but I have a sneaking feeling it's not.

I turn, take a deep breath, open my eyes and see…Davis. I look at him questioningly. Then I exhale in total relief.

His eyes are already open. He looks at me softly, "Good morning, Alcohol Bunny."

I don't want to lift my head, pretty sure that if I do, I'll be very sorry. "Oh, shit, I got good and wasted last night, didn't I?"

"Ummmhmmm."

"Did I do anything stupid? Did we???" I point back and forth between us.

"Not really stupid… and no, we didn't." I believe him.

"Why are you here?"

"I found you passed out at the party." I notice he is still wearing his TRICK t-shirt and recall seeing it last night. "Brought you home, cleaned you up a bit and put you to bed. I thought I should stay in case you woke up sick or confused."

"Did I vomit?"

Davis shakes his head no, but indicates "a little" with his thumb and forefinger.

"I am so sorry you had to see that." I prop my head up on my hand to check to see how badly I'm going to feel when I get up. It hurts. This is going to suck.

"It's okay, happens to the best of us. I only took your clothes off because I didn't think you'd want to sleep in them after you... you know." He mimes barfing. "I think you ruined your fuzzy slippers." *Oh, crap, Suzette's Uggs!*

"How come you brought me home? Where's Jake?"

"I couldn't find him," Davis says a bit angrily. Then changing his tone to one full of concern, adds, "And you really needed to get to bed."

Moaning while falling back onto my pillow, I tell him, "Thanks again. My head hurts and I want to die." This makes Davis laugh.

"Ow!" I say, folding my arms across my face and covering my ears.

"Sorry."

Davis tells me I need coffee and carbs. He runs down to the coffee stand to get some. I clean up in my bathroom while he is gone.

When he returns we sit on my bed leaning against the wall and he recalls my evening for me. The way he describes it and from what I can remember, it sounds like I had a really good time, until I didn't. He suddenly gets very serious, "Lizard Breath?"

"Yeah, Mavis?'

"Can I ask you to do something for me?"

"Sure. Anything."

"Could you please not get that drunk again without me or Jules or Charlie around to take care of you?"

"I don't think I'll ever get that drunk again. I am regretting it today. But, yes, I promise, I will not drink without a buddy in the future."

Davis repeats the word "Buddy," softly, takes a sip of his coffee, chuckles a bit and shakes his head. He reaches over, grabs my phone from my nightstand and begins scrolling through my contacts. "Okay, Charlie...aaand Jules." He's reading through my contacts to make sure I have phone numbers in case I get drunk again. "Hmm, no Davis OR Mavis. Well, we can fix that right now." He punches something into my phone and then hands it to me.

It reads: DAVIS/MAVIS/ICE and then his number.

113

"ICE?" I ask, confused.

"In Case of Emergency."

"You're my 'In Case of Emergency?'

Davis gives me a pleased nod. *He's my In Case of Emergency.*

CHAPTER 11: NOW-November

Since the Halloween party, I'm enjoying even more attention than I got when I was RA of the all guys floor. I still have Chinese food one night a week with Charlie and Jake. I like those dinners best when Jules can join us. They are like double dates. Game Nights continue, when I can make it. I am much busier at The Space since Othello opens the week after Thanksgiving. I know Jake goes to Game Night religiously. I think he is helping Suzette out with the organization of them when he doesn't practice with Boxwood. More than all the activity, though, I always have an escort back to the dorms at the end of every evening at The Space. One or two times a week, Jake is there as I finish up. He will help me with the last few things and then we walk to Lawrence. A few times he brought Suzette with him. I prefer when he doesn't, because when he's alone he walks me to my door and some nights comes in for a while. He's been much more physical since Halloween, but not to the point where I feel uncomfortable. I wonder to myself how long he will wait before he pushes to go further than making out. We've gotten to the point where shirts have come off and there is considerable groping. I wonder how much longer *I* can wait. I have to admit, all the macking on each other is getting me more than a bit riled up.

Davis always checks, every night, to make sure I'm okay. If he sees Jake there, he generally winks at me and leaves. It makes me a little sad. Most nights, though, it's Davis that comes to collect me and take me home. I'm always so happy to see him. I anticipate his small touches and friendly hugs so much. I feel anxious and can't relax until he nudges my shoulder in jest or picks up my chin to tell me something. One of the things I look forward to the most is when Davis comes to get me and I'm listening to my iPod not paying attention. He will slowly come up behind me. And I know it's him, without even a glance over my shoulder. I can sense it when he comes into a room. He'll gently cup both my shoulders with his hands and pull me back, and husk into my ear, "Ready to roll?" He has no idea how ready. Davis has me completely on edge. I keep thinking about what he said about asking for what I want.

I know it's not exactly cool, since he is with Kathleen and Jake is being so sweet, but neither one of us seem to want or know how to stop. Since he lives off campus, Davis generally drives me the few blocks to the dorm. The electrical zap is magnified when we are sitting side by side in his SUV. I can't believe he can't hear my heart bumping around in my chest. If he accidently touches my arm to get my attention or pushes my hair off my face to check my expression, I have to squeeze my legs together or squirm around in my seat, his proximity is so…SO.

Tuesday before Thanksgiving is a partial dress/tech rehearsal of Othello. I already informed Jake it would be a late night, so he is not coming to get me. He told me the band is having a final rehearsal tonight before the short time off we have for Thanksgiving, so he'll be busy with that. It's after midnight when Davis shows up in the costume shop. He looks pale and exhausted.

"You look seriously beat." I tell him.

"I am and I have to drive home tomorrow." We hadn't talked about plans for Thanksgiving. I am staying in town. I'm not up for the trip home and I really don't want to endure my parents watching me like a hawk the entire time I'm there—monitoring my sleep and eating and every move like I'm about to fall apart. Like last summer. I'm staying here and having an "Orphan's Thanksgiving" with Mel and Kris at their apartment. I think Suzette and Smitty might be coming, too. Jake is driving home. Jules is taking Charlie to meet her parents and is a complete wreck about it. I can't wait to hear how that goes. Bringing a rock singer home for turkey, ha! She lives in one of the outer suburbs of the city so I'll probably see them over the weekend, too.

I hadn't known, about Davis' plans, until just now.

"I know home is in Illinois. How far away?"

"Outside of Chicago. Kathleen is texting me every hour on the hour. My mom is so excited to see me. I haven't seen her or my father since the beginning of the semester. I think mom can't wait for me to get there so she can have a break."

"A break from what?"

There is a long pause. I wait for Davis to elaborate. After a few weight shifts in his seat and rubbing his hands across the steering wheel he finally begins, "I don't talk about it much, Lizard…" Slowly, painfully Davis divulges details about home. His dad is in a wheelchair. He is a quadriplegic with partial use of his arms. Some sort of accident. Davis can't or won't elaborate. I had no idea. I don't push for more as it appears to be upsetting him.

"That's why I am a bit older than the average Weldon student. It happened at the end of my senior year in high school. I delayed college to stay home and help my mom with him… and stuff."

If I wasn't already a big fan of Davis', that statement shoved me right into super fangirl status. He is way more than gorgeous and talented. He might be one of the sweetest, most responsible people I know.

"There is no other family to help out?"

"No, I had a brother, but…he…died." Davis' words start to sound strained. I think he is tearing up. It kills me to see him like this and I slide over closer to him, turn into him and hold him. He lets me and soon his head is on my chest. I feel him gasp for breath, trying to keep from crying, I think.

119

"Cole?" I ask.

"How did you know his name was Cole?"

"I guessed. I've seen your tattoo. I have wondered about it, but didn't want to ask. Mostly since I'm not supposed to be looking at your chest and also because you never volunteered."

He pulls away to look at me and in a deep voice with an edge of tease, says, "You've been looking at my chest?" Still emotional, he wipes at his eyes and smirks, trying to distract me from a conversation that is obviously difficult.

I am not going to let him go off track. "Stop. Stop embarrassing me. Stop deflecting. Talk to me."

We sit there a bit more, my head on his shoulder, holding hands, as he calms himself and finally says, "It's a really long, ugly story, Biz. There still isn't an ending. There probably never will be. I... I don't think I can go into the whole thing tonight. Someday." I let it go. That will have to be enough for me for now. I really don't want to push him and it's really late.

"So, no Jake for the weekend?" he says, changing the subject none too subtly. I shake my head no. "So, no action, huh?" he questions sarcastically. What? What is Davis saying?

"Not that it's any of your business." I snap.

"What? I was just saying… I thought…since… I mean you and Jake are together a lot… he takes you home a lot."

"So do you, Davis." My temper is rising. Obnoxiously, I continue, "What about you… what about Kathleen? It will be some kind of reunion, won't it? I mean, you haven't seen each other in weeks? That's gotta get to a guy? And I've heard you've cut down on your extra-curricular sex this semester. I'm sure you'll barely see the outside of her bedroom." I have never spoken to Davis like that, but I'm frankly mad at his insinuations and well, jealous. I want to hurt him. I remove my head from his shoulder and am sitting up straight.

I am expecting him to yell at me. Call me a bitch. He doesn't. Davis says softly and almost apologetically, "She's my girlfriend, Lizard." Glancing over, I see him swallow hard a couple of times. Then he adds, "I'm sorry I said anything about you and Jake. You're right, I have no right to pry. I like you, so much. I just don't want to think about you with… about you hurt again, ever."

I pull my hand away and slide back to the passenger side of the car. "I'm working on that, Mavis. Not getting hurt. And I like you, too. You might be my best friend. Thank you for caring about me. If

121

you weren't wi…" I can't finish that thought. I try to wordlessly wave it off with my hand, but I am dying inside. I know he is going to sleep with Kathleen while he's gone. Why wouldn't he? They are engaged. I hate it. And I wish I didn't. And I wish he was mine.

"If I weren't what?" he pursues, taking my hand back and rubbing his thumb across my knuckles.

"Hers," I whisper so quietly he can't hear. Collecting myself, I turn and tell him, "Never mind."

"Have a good Thanksgiving, Mavis," I say forlornly, looking at his amazing green eyes.

He reaches over and puts his hand on the side of my face and I lean into it. "You too, Lizard Breath." Then he leans over and kisses me softly on the other cheek. It feels like more than just a "see ya" good-bye. The thought saddens me. "You, too," he repeats.

Thanksgiving Day comes and goes. I go through all the motions of being a good guest at Kris and Mel's. We eat a delicious, if not slightly bizarre, meal. It's a potluck and everyone has brought something that is traditional from their own Thanksgivings back home. Mel, being from the south, has brought corn casserole and bourbon sweet potatoes. The strangest thing is a strawberry-pretzel jello salad, which sounds gross, but is surprisingly awesome. Smitty's contribution. Charlie notices my mood. When he asks I tell him I'm homesick. But really I'm boy sick. Jake sick. And terribly, terribly Davis sick. Dammit.

I muddle through the rest of the holiday weekend, looking out for the residents that have stayed over in the dorms for the holiday. We are short staffed for the weekend, so I am looking after several floors and am on call for Saturday and Sunday. I take the time to clean my room, do the back load of laundry I have and write a paper for Linguistics. It's almost enough to keep my mind off Davis. I think about Jake, too. I ponder what I am doing with him. Why I am with him? Why do I think more about Davis than Jake? Logically, it doesn't make sense to be thinking of Davis so much. I guess relationships aren't really logical are they?

Monday is a relief. I'm happy to be back to a normal schedule to fill up my time and my too-busy mind. Classes are getting down to the wire with projects and papers. We are in tech for Othello the first four days of this week and open on Friday. Things with Davis seem, okay. A little tense. Not as lighthearted. Jake has made a point of picking me up every night from The Space. I notice that Davis hasn't even come by to check on me. I confess, I'm disappointed. I see him talking animatedly on the phone during the tech rehearsal intermissions. I just know it's Kathleen. He seems excited and a bit agitated, but he occasionally laughs and smiles. His laughs and smiles are for Kathleen, not me. He hasn't touched me or really smiled at me since he got back. Jake, on the other hand, is super attentive. He holds my hand whenever he can. He gives me little kisses on the cheek and by my ears. When I am alone with Jake, I find myself dreaming it's Davis instead of him. It's these thoughts of Davis that trigger my physical responses. It's so pathetic. I have to get over this Davis hang-up. It's almost like the more I push it away the more it stays. And it's not fair to Jake.

Chapter 12: NOW-November/December

Othello opens to much acclaim. It deserves it. The actors, especially the ones playing Othello and Iago, are superb. The sets are simple and elegant. Davis' lighting makes them shine. I never thought much about sound design, but after hanging around this production, I have a bigger appreciation. It was excellent. After the curtain comes down and the actors have left, I use one of their dressing rooms to change for the opening night party. Nothing over the top, just a little black dress with a huge red silk rose on one shoulder and my prize possession—black Christian Louboutin pumps with red soles. I saved a long time for them. I could have bought six or seven dresses for the price of them and I love them. I pass the "PJ test,"

when he checks out my outfit and deems it worthy.

When I ask him, "Really?" all he say is, "Bizzy, Gays don't lie

about fashion."

In exaggerated faux shock I exclaim,

"What?...You...You're...Gay???"

I've got PJ giggling. He teases right back and in his "butch-

est" voice replies, "Damn, girl, and I thought I was hiding it so well."

PJ turns as a guest enters. Jake has arrived in the costume shop. He is

wearing "the Jake look." Vintage grey suit, white shirt, skinny tie. He

could be on the cover of a jazz album.

"Well, hello handsome," PJ says to greet Jake, "butch-voice"

now completely abandoned. PJ pouts a little air kiss to me as he exits.

"You have fun tonight, Miss Bizzy."

"You, too, PJ...can't wait to see your ensemble."

Jake clears his throat to get my attention. "You look great,

Bizzy," Jake compliments.

"You clean up pretty good yourself, Mr., Gianni."

I gather my sparkly clutch purse and take Jake's arm to head

out to the party at The Lum. I've already told myself I am not going to drink tonight. The Halloween party taught me a lesson. I am going to carry a red cup, but drink water. That way everyone will leave me alone about drinking, and I can have a good time. Peer pressure still exists after you turn 21.

I have also told myself I am going to focus on Jake and quit with all the mind chatter about Davis. *He's just a friend and can be nothing more. Nothing more.* I find myself in need of my mantra, something I haven't consciously needed in a while. *I can do this. I can so totally do this. I can do this. I can do this.* I need it more than I thought.

It's only minutes before Jake and I run into Davis. And of course, he looks devastatingly handsome tonight. I've never seen him more attractive, probably because I've never seen him so dressed up. Who am I kidding? I think he looks hot in anything. He is wearing a sharp, fitted black suit and a crisp white shirt with no tie. The suit is well made. Expensive. His hair is combed back slightly away from his face and his eyes...Whoa... they are greener than ever. Maybe it's because I've forced myself not to look at him over the past week. Maybe it's missing him. His beautiful face just crushes me.

Then I see he's not alone. "Lizar..." he stops himself before he calls me by his nickname for me. "Biz...Jake... this is my fiancée, Kathleen." We all shake hands. Jake makes a point of telling her "how very nice it is to finally meet Davis' girl." I would be cold and snippy, but Kathleen is too nice. Beautiful thick, long, dark, dark brown flowing hair draped over one shoulder and dark brown eyes. My eyes are a unimpressive grey-green color. Hazel, I guess people call it. Every time I hear "Hazel," I think of a witch, so I call them grey-green. Kathleen looks so glamorous compared to me. And tall, dammit. Where I am petite and curvy, she is tall and statuesque. In her heels, she is almost as tall as Davis. I barely come up to anyone's chin.

"Biz, it is so good to meet you. Davis loves working with you. He is always telling me funny stories about you." *Oh, yeah, that's me. The funny "friend."*

"You, too. Yeah, Mavis is great," I say half-heartedly. Broken heartedly. I notice she pinches her eyebrows together when I say "Mavis," but says nothing.

This isn't working. I am dying inside. Focus. Focus on Jake.

Jake jumps into the conversation and is quickly occupying Kathleen's attention, quizzing her about music and telling her about Boxwood.

I feel, rather than see, Davis slightly to my side, "You look really pretty," he whispers down, brushing his lips near my ear. I stay facing Jake and Kathleen, but push my lips together to keep from inhaling or sobbing, I don't know which.

"Thank you," I reply almost voiceless. His breath and touch so near to me make me shake. I feel the familiar warm sensation heating up in my heart and beginning to move lower. I'm surprised the whole room doesn't feel it. He touches my elbow briefly. When he removes his hand, I miss his touch immediately. Davis moves to collect his fiancée from Jake.

Jake and I make our way around the party. Every now and then, I catch sight of Davis and Kathleen. He is whispering in her ear and holding her hand. She smiles up at him with a smile I recognize. It's how I imagine I look at him sometimes. I make up my mind to stop looking at them…him, for the rest of the night. I decide to act like I am having a great time in hopes that I eventually really will. I wrap myself around Jake, nuzzle his ear, give him quick kisses. He seems really pleased and lights up with every bit of affection I give him. Perhaps I have been holding back too much. He IS very sweet. He slowly walks me out to the front porch. I like him touching the small of my back to lead me out the front door. We walk slowly over to the corner of the porch by a large pillar in between two railings. He turns in front of me to lean against the pillar and pulls me to him, sliding his hand from my back to my waist.

Looking me pointedly in the eyes, he touches my chin with his index finger, "Do you know how hard it is to get alone time with you?" I shake my head. "And do you have any idea how hot you look tonight?" Again, I shake my head no. "I swear I saw at least ten guys looking at you." His hand has moved to my hair and the one on my waist is pulling me closer. I have all but forgotten about Davis. Davis and Kathleen. His hand in my hair at the back of my neck, Jake pulls my face toward him for a kiss. I place both my hands on his chest. I'm ready, either way, to give in or push away, I haven't decided quite yet. Then I feel his lips on mine and I just want to wipe away the sad I feel about Davis. And the stupidity I feel about liking him. So I give in. To Jake. To myself. And I kiss him, letting him part my lips and slip his tongue in. I even sigh in the relief of letting go. I'm sure Jake takes it for passion. We are standing so close, my thighs are straddling his as we lean against the pillar. I am just at the point of caving to the physical sensations that are creeping up on me and pushing myself right into him.

"Oh, that is so cute," I hear a girl's voice say. It stops me from continuing to kiss Jake. He is still going, but I'm paralyzed. I pull away from him and turn just my head toward the voice. It's Kathleen. And Davis is right next to her, putting his jacket around her shoulders as they head out of the party. Freezing where he stands; he pierces me with his stare. His eyebrows come together and the corners of his lips move down in a frown. Never releasing my gaze, he leans down and whispers into Kathleen's ear. When he comes up from the whisper, he looks at Jake quickly. Jake is mumbling something to me about ignoring them, but I don't hear him. I am like a moth to the flame, being pulled into Davis' emerald eyes. I feel the pull I always do, but it feels heavier, almost dangerous now.

"Jake," Davis says, acknowledging him with a growl. "Can I speak with Biz a second, it's a Space thing."

"Can't it wait, Davis?" I ask, a bit annoyed. I was just getting to a point where I was going to let Jake help me forget Davis and Bam!, there he is.

"No, Biz," He insists, "It can't."

Stepping backward and away, I apologize to Jake and stride toward Davis. He doesn't touch me, but somehow herds me to the other end of the porch, leaving Jake to entertain Kathleen. She looks confused.

When he finally stops and turns me around by the elbow, releasing it quickly, it's obvious he is mad. In an angry whisper he snaps out at me, "What the fuck are you doing?" I shake my head in confusion and scowl at him, "I'm kissing my date. My... my boyfriend."

"Are you drunk?"

"No."

"Do you really know what you are doing tonight?" Davis questions.

I don't respond.

"Biz... Lizard Breath...Baby, what are you thinking?"

And for the first time all night, I am honest with myself. "I don't know what I'm thinking. Don't call me Baby or Lizard Breath. Don't. Not anymore. Ever. You're...You're with her. And I...I'm gonna be with Jake."

"Is that what you want?"

I can't have what I want. I say the first part of the thought to myself, but inadvertently say, "What I want," out loud. I add sarcastically, "It's what you told me I should do."

Davis' mouth opens in shock and he's about to say something in retort, when I run over and grab Jake's hand, telling him it's time to go. I march off the porch with Jake following me, confused. I turn one last time and say loudly, "Come on Jake, let's go back to the dorm." As I say it I look right into Davis' eyes. He is speechless and appears defeated. Good. Now he knows how I've felt all night. How I've felt every night since he left for Thanksgiving.

Tugging Jake's hand, we barrel down the few blocks to the dorm from The Lum. He's asking me questions non-stop.

"What the hell was that? What did he say?

I turn quickly, so quickly Jake has to grab my arms to keep me from falling backward on my ass like an idiot.

"Hey, what the fuck, Biz?" he asks again.

I lie. "Davis is sticking his nose in and giving advice where none is needed." Then I add a bit of the truth, "He's so damn perfect and righteous."

Jake snorts. "He's far from perfect. And he's giving YOU advice? About what? Us? Me?" Jake questions with a less than thrilled tone.

"Just....just stuff," I lie again. A lie of omission. Finally, coming down from my anger I add, "It's frustrating." Because it is.

"Screw Davis!" Jake pulls me toward him with a rapid movement and covers my mouth with his in a series of kisses in between which he states, "He... should... pay... attention... to his girl... and leave mine alone."

I'm Jake's girl? Do I want to be "Jake's Girl?"

Extracting my lips from Jake's mouth to contemplate what he just said, I see the large black Cadillac Escalade pull up next to us on the street. It slows briefly enough for Davis' eyes to make contact with mine and burn right into my soul before speeding up and tearing out of sight.

Well, I'm definitely not DAVIS' girl.

134

I give my full attention back to Jake and his lips, that in the time I spied the car have traveled down my neck. Jake was totally unaware of Davis' car.

"Hmm, you smell so good, Biz, " he huskily says into my ear.

I am keyed up, angry, frustrated and yes, turned on, in a bizarre way. How dare Davis question me? He doesn't have to be alone tonight. He is going home with Miss Sweet and Perfect. I'm alone. A lot. I've been alone since Neil screwed me over. No... before that... I was an only child. As an adult, I've been alone since I can remember. Friends, but nobody that was mine. No real boyfriend. No real love. I'm sick of it.

My body is reacting to Jake's attentions, but I am way inside my head.

Jake doesn't notice I'm not really there, since my body is acting like it is. "Should we go to my room, Biz?" Jake asks, pulling me out of my dreaming/moping.

"Sure... Yeah."

I can't get Davis' voice out of my mind, *"Do you really know what you are doing tonight? Is that what you want?"*

What AM I doing?

135

When we get to the landing of the second floor of Lawrence, Jake turns me quickly and pushes me up against the wall. He apparently can't wait to get to his room to start. He trails hot, soft kisses from right below my ear, down my neck and across my collarbone to my shoulder. Reaching down he pulls my knee up to his hip, positioning his now obvious erection right between my legs. He slides up my body. Oh, hell. I haven't been touched like this in so long. Jake has been beyond patient and he is kind to me. I tilt my pelvis, pushing into his hardness, when…

WAAWAAWAAWAAAWAAWAAWAAWAAAWAAA. The fire alarm goes off.

It stops our movement. My eyes widen as I push him off. My mind flies immediately to my RA duties in an emergency and off my current position on the stairs with Jake. Ignoring situations like fire drills is what almost lost me my RA job last year. I can't screw up again.

"Hey, I gotta go," I yell at Jake as I leave and run up the stairs to my floor. "Get to your floor's meeting place."

Running up the stairs I see several of the fifth floor residents scrambling down. I make mental notes of who I've seen. Once on five I move quickly down the hall, knocking on every door. It's after midnight. Some sound sleepers might not have awoken to the alarm. In the hall the noise is deafening and the seizure-inducing lights are flashing in rhythm with the alarm. I wake a few people and move them along. Funny. I haven't seen or smelled any smoke, but that doesn't mean anything. My emergency training has taught me it could be electrical or in a different part of the building. It doesn't matter, fire spreads quickly.

If nobody answers the door I'm knocking on, I take my master key and unlock it to make sure the room is clear. Once I know there is no one left on the floor, I head down to the pre-determined meeting spot for my floor on the south side of the building. Odd numbered floor residents meet on the south, even floors on the north. I'm sure Jake is with his floor on the other side of the building.

Any excitement I so recently felt to be with Jake is gone, replaced with concern and responsibility for my peers. Many of the residents are in pajamas; some with no shoes. A few couples are even naked and wrapped up in blankets. Looking around, I spot Jules and Charlie. They are one of the blanket couples. I chuckle to myself.

Figures. I am also relieved that they are safe. Fire alarms going off and mandatory evacuation is one way to find out who is hooking up.

It's a good fifteen minutes out in the cold November night air before the Fire Marshall calls the all clear, letting us know it's safe to return to our rooms.

Tired, cold and still a bit dazed from the excitement of the fire alarm, not to mention my run-in with Davis and making out with Jake, I don't even look for Jake on the way in. I need to make sure my floor is settled and that any students accidently locked out in the rush of evacuation can get into their room.

Finally back in my room for the night, I flop myself into my bed, squirming and wiggling out of my clothes, too tired to do it standing up. Jake hasn't called or texted. No knock on my door. Guess he just went to bed. I am asleep in no time.

***

Tuesday's RA staff meeting includes a debriefing about the fire alarm. The rumor going around is that some of the international students were cooking in the dorm kitchens and a grease fire broke out.

The official report is that a pull station on the first floor near the front entrance to the dorm was activated. There are no signs of smoke or fire damage in that area.

Chapter 13: NOW-December

The run of Othello feels like it has gone by fast. I no longer have either of my escorts home at night. Jake is either too busy getting ready for finals or at Boxwood practice, and Davis... Davis is staying far away from me. He is professional when we interact at The Space, but the lightheartedness is gone. He hasn't called me Lizard Breath since I told him not to. I feel like I've lost my best friend. I know it's about Jake, making out with Jake in front of him at the party. He thinks I slept with Jake and he seems pissed or disappointed in me or something. I keep trying to think of ways to talk to him about it. I just can't seem to find the right moment. If I do talk to him about it, I'll sound like an idiot. I'm sure he took Kathleen home and had sex with her opening night, so I don't know why he is being cold to me. It's all so tense and awkward now. I don't know what to do.

The Sunday afternoon the show closes I have a dinner break before I have to go back and help with "strike," the taking down of the production of Othello. It's when all the sets are removed and disassembled, the costumes cleaned and returned to storage and the props put away. I haven't really hung out with Jake, except in the cafeteria at lunch. He told me that after the fire alarm went off and he finally got back to his room, he just fell asleep. I have no reason not to believe him. I did the same thing. I catch myself wondering if we really are "into this"… whatever "this" is? If we really were, wouldn't we be desperate to see each other? I decide that before I head out to The Space, I will find him and apologize. Maybe "course correct" a little since we were interrupted by the alarm. I text him several times, but get no response. I don't have a lot of time to wait around, so I gather my bag and things for strike. I swing by his room on the chance he is there to at least start a conversation. After knocking on his door a few times, the door next to his opens. His suite mate tells me he's not home. That he hasn't been there for a few days, at least while the suite mate has been there.

"Okay, thanks for letting me know. If you see him, can you tell him Biz is looking for him?" I request.

"No problem."

I check the turrets, just in case there is a Sunday Game Afternoon going on. Nobody is there, so I head down the hall to the main staircase.

With one foot on the stairs to head out to The Space, I decide to text Jake one more time. A few seconds after I push SEND, I hear a phone's alert tone. It sounds like Jake's. His tone is very distinctive. I've heard it before. That's so weird. Probably just a coincidence. But then it alerts again. I follow the alert noise. It leads me to the door of Suzette's room. My hand goes up to knock, when I hear the very obvious sounds of people having sex. Suzette having sex. And Jake's phone is in there? I am paralyzed outside the room. Jake and Suzette? *No, it's a coincidence. Suzette probably just has the same alert tone.* There's one thing I can try and then I'll be sure. I pull out my phone and call Jake. I rarely call anyone except my parents and Jules, mostly I just text. I don't know his ringtone. But, again, a few seconds after sending, I hear a phone ringing in Suzette's room. I hear scrambling in the room and the ringing stops. GODDAMNIT.

142

Again!! It's happening to me again. I am such a fool. A trusting, ridiculous fool.

Frozen in front of Suzette's door, I begin to weep. They could open it at any time and see me. I gotta get out of here. I sniffle and wipe at my eyes. I am in shock. REALLY, Again? It's all I can process. I move and am halfway down the first flight, when I hear the door open. Good, they didn't see me.

"It was Biz. I have a few texts and she just called." I hear Jake say to Suzette.

"What are you going to say to her?"

"That I was talking to you…" and then Jake sees me, evidently, because right as I hit the landing below and am almost out of sight he yells down at me, "Hey, Bizzy..." I can hear the fakeness in his voice. " I just got your messages." *Yeah, I know you did.* "What's up?" I see Suzette come out and stand beside him and whisper something I can't hear.

"Uh, nothing urgent." I pause on the stairs and yell back up, plastering on a fake smile and utilizing the calmest voice I can muster.

Jake starts to explain, "Sorry, I missed them. I was just…talking… to…Suz."

143

I don't want to hear it. I yell up at them, "It's cool, I'll talk to you later. I gotta get to The Space for strike."

I refuse to let them see me fall apart. I have moved out of their visual range, but I can hear them talking to each other above me. I can't really make out anything other than Suzette saying, "with Davis," and then the door closing. With Davis? What the hell does that mean? Was she with Davis, too? Does she think I was with Davis? I mentally kick myself the entire walk to The Space. DAMMIT. This is just the type of thing I did not want to happen this year. Exactly what I'd planned to avoid. In trying to look and act normal, I'd gotten myself into another triangle. Almost to the costume shop, I can't stop the tears from coming. They are part sadness and another part total frustration and anger at myself. I know better. Have I learned nothing? Am I worried about my feelings, my lack of control, or what others will think? Getting to the costume shop, I close the door behind me and throw my stuff on the table.

"Biz?...What's going on? The door was closed... Are you okay?" Davis asks me softly. After my awkward and suspicious meet-up with Jake and Suzette on the stairs outside of her room, I have retreated to stand in the corner of The Space's laundry/costume/all-purpose area to lick my wounds. I am looking up at a light above me. I've heard if you look up with your eyes only when you want to cry it will help you stop. It isn't working. Tears are popping out of my eyes and running down my cheeks. I'm pretty sure I look... Awesome. Awesomely red nosed and snotty. It's an ugly cry, but, thankfully, not loud. Davis has moved toward me, I can feel him behind me and off to my left. I am feeling conflicted. I want him here. I don't want him here. Why is he being sweet to me now, after being so cold all week? I want to see him and have him hug me or hold my hand. That need seems hypocritical after my suspicions about Jake and Suzette. I push down the guilt.

Sort of squatting down in front of me to meet me at teary eye level and wrapping his hand gently around my elbow, Davis again asks, "Hey, you okay?" I relax the minute he touches me. Just his voice and the look of concern in his soulful green eyes set me off. I immediately throw my arms around his waist and bury my face in his chest, as he stands to catch me. I sort of fall into him. I have missed him so much.

"I am an idiot. . .How could I let myself be made such a fool of again? I must have some sort of sticker on me that says, "'Please cheat and whore around on me.'""

Davis pulls my face up from his chest with his hands. He wipes away my tears with both of his thumbs while holding my face. "What? What are you talking about? You're not a…" I describe everything I witnessed with Jake and Suzette. Spill out the whole scene. The noises. The cell phone ringing. Suzette's insinuating tone when I overheard her say "with Davis." He is shaking his head in disbelief. He pulls me into him, wrapping his arms around me, as I sob. He is stroking my back with his thumbs. I like it so much when he does that. I pull away and look deep into his eyes. Davis is here. HE is holding me. HE is comforting me. HE is the one… that has leaned down and is softly kissing the tears on my lips away.

"Biz…no."

It feels so right. Just like his hugs and touches always have. Our kissing deepens. Davis' tongue parts my lips. And I let him. He licks my upper lip and then my lower lip before running his tongue across mine. I let out a soft groaning hum and he reciprocates. I pull him in tighter to me. He responds, his hands firmly on my hips and

146

then moves them around to cup my bottom. Kissing him is wiping away all the pain and uncertainty of a moment ago. I can feel how excited he is against my stomach. That causes an hot achy throb to develop between my legs. Pulling each other closer, rocking in rhythm against one another, we both hum aloud with pleasure.

Then, suddenly Davis pulls away, holding me slightly away from him, "What are you doing, Biz?" he asks.

"What do you mean…What am *I* doing?…What are *you* doing?" I reply and blink away tears.

He looks me dead in the eyes, "No…I can't." He turns quickly, his arms tense and his hands balled in fists. He's on the move before I can get a thought from my head to my mouth, like *Stop, Wait….Don't leave…Talk to me… I don't want you to leave. I want you. I WANT my friend. I WANT YOU, DAVIS.* As this realization takes hold, he is gone. I am just standing there, paralyzed by my thoughts. Aching for him to come back. I know what I want.

Chapter 14: NOW-Winter Break

Winter break starts in two days, but Davis is conspicuously absent from The Space, from the cafeteria, from Weldon. He hasn't been around since yesterday. . .and the kissing. . . .and the leaving. I wonder where he is. Why he left so suddenly. Did he take his finals? He is supposed to graduate this semester. Will that still happen? I don't ask. Nobody says a word about his whereabouts. They are all too busy packing up to go home for the holidays.

Most of the two days, I hide out in my room. I sneak into the cafeteria one time each day around lunch, after I know Suzette is gone. Jake hasn't been around, thankfully. Jules usually texts me with the all-clear. She knows all about the Jake and Suzette issue. She knows I am avoiding. When I get to the cafeteria, Jules moves down for me, moving closer to Charlie. He says, "Hey." Jules is my friend and Charlie is Jake's. It makes this all kinds of awkward.

Jules asks, "Biz. How are you doing? What's your plan for winter break…and stuff?" And stuff. Meaning, what's going on with Jake. I don't think she has a clue about my kissing Davis. I haven't told her. I feel really alone. A few days ago, I had what I thought was a boyfriend and a best friend. Jake wasn't really a boyfriend, I am coming to realize. I don't really know what Davis means to me. I just know I want him around. All the time. I am confused. Now, they are both gone.

"My plan, Jules, is to pack up and go home for the holidays. I haven't thought much beyond that. I don't want to talk to Jake yet. I want to act like nothing happened. I wish I could find Da…" I cut myself off before I accidentally say Davis' name. "So, I go home, act normal and don't freak my parents out. I think I did enough of that last year. THAT is my plan."

"Let me know how that works out for you," Jules smirks. "No, really, keep in touch, call me, text me. If you can't keep up the façade for your folks, run away for a coffee and call me." Giving her a sideways hug and swallowing a couple of times, I squeak out, "Thanks, Jules. You know I will."

Home is four hours away by car, but I don't have a car. My parents gave me the choice of the bus and Christmas presents or the plane and none. I chose the plane. It's a one-hour flight. I don't need any extra time to mope before I get home and have to slap on the "fake face" for almost three weeks. I have been moping for the past few days. Every time I went into the cafeteria or walk down the halls to a final I rely on my mantra. *I can do this. I can SO do this.* Sometimes I would add a "Totally" if I was feeling especially fragile. *I can SO totally do this.*

My parents meet me at the airport by baggage claim. Dad asks me how my flight was.

I tell him, "Fine," because it was uneventful and really all I was doing was feeling sad, lonely and stupid the entire flight. Mom tells me I look a little tired. I blame it on finals and packing. It will be nice to be home for a while and not have things around that remind me of Jake… or Davis. Things that remind me of how I seem to be repeating my pattern of stupidity from last year when I swore to myself I

150

wouldn't. Actually being at home sort of DOES remind me of last year's failures.

Chapter 15: THEN-Last Summer

The girl my father picked up in front of Merten Hall last spring was like something you scrape off the bottom of your shoe. Dirty. Flattened. Unrecognizable, if you didn't already know her. After he greeted me with a concerned look and a hug...

"Hi, Biz kid."

"Hi, Daddy."

The questions began. I gave vague, half-hearted replies.

He kept it up for about an hour and then just gave up and allowed me to stay quiet, looking out the passenger window for the remainder of the trip. He knew something was very wrong, but he didn't pursue it. My dad was intuitive like that when it came to me.

My mother wasn't quite so chill. She was hovering by the door for my return. I came into the house and practically slammed right into her. She pulled me into a hug and I hugged her back, but not too hard. If I gave in and hugged back too much, I would shatter into a million pieces. I pulled away and gave her a tight smile, holding back tears, straightened my bag over my shoulder and marched down to my room in the lower level.

I heard her greet my dad, "Cal, is she okay?" and his reply, "No, I don't think so." How right he was.

Finally reaching my bedroom at home, it felt as if I had been holding my breath for hours. I exhaled and fell to my knees on the floor. Kicking the door shut with my foot, I crawled to the bed and climbed under the covers fully dressed. I never turned on the light. The crying began immediately. It only increased when I realized my mother had made my bed for me, because the sheets were so soft and smelled so good. I must have cried myself to sleep. I remember waking to my mother stroking my hair and face.

Looking at me with eyebrows raised in concern, she said, "I don't know what happened to you, sweetie. Whatever it is you're safe now. Do you want to come up and have some dinner with Dad and me?"

"I don't think so, Mom. I just want to sleep."

"Okay."

Mom let me sleep until noon the next day. I know I wasn't asleep that whole time, but in and out. When I wasn't sleeping my brain would go into overdrive, replaying everything, beginning with Neil's rejection, on an endless loop. My only reprieve was to sleep, so I'd force myself under again. When Mom woke me, she told me I didn't have to tell her or Dad anything. They loved me and they wanted me to be well. Hearing that, without any of the judgment I was throwing on myself was my undoing. I threw my arms around her and cried for what seems like an eternity. I couldn't talk. I just cried. And she rocked me. Finally, Mom told me she'd made an appointment for me with a counselor. I needed to talk to someone. She was right. It wasn't until tomorrow, but until then she was going to baby me. It was all so kind and gentle, like she knew I was super fragile. Mom helped me up out of bed, picked out some comfy pajamas from my

154

drawer and walked me into my bathroom. She started a bath and left, telling me to come upstairs and have something to eat when I was done.

I washed and conditioned my hair and scrubbed my body with the bath puff using my favorite apple body wash. When the thought loop would try to play, I would submerge my head under the water and hold my breath. I stayed in the bathtub until the water got cold. Getting out, I dried my body and towel dried and combed my hair. I couldn't take the noise of the blow dryer. The pajamas my mother had chosen smelled like my sheets, like home. A sense that I was in a safe place started to leak in. I had been on the edge for the past few weeks, on alert and trying to squash and control every feeling. I knew I went about it all the wrong way. I just needed a little guidance on how to get back to me, the right way.

Climbing the stairs to the upper level of my house, my mouth watered at the smell of chicken and dumplings. It's not something my Mom would normally make in the summer, but I think she knew it would be comforting and I would eat it. Entering the large space that was the family room, kitchen and dining room, she encouraged me to sit on the sofa and wrap up in some blankets. I was visibly shaky.

That's what happens when you are trying to hold yourself together and are finally slowly letting things go. I sat and ate a small bowl of the chicken and dumplings. It tasted better than anything I'd had in a year. Mom turned on the television. I made her click past anything remotely dramatic or sexual. We eventually wound up watching a documentary about penguins. It was about all I could handle. We sat in the family room and barely talked, but it was comforting. Mom let me fall asleep on the couch sometime during the afternoon. I didn't wake up until the next morning. I didn't have to endure the thought loop even once all night.

The next morning, my Dad came into the family room just as I was waking.

"Biz kid, I'm going to drive you to the counselor," he told me.

"I'm pretty sure I can drive myself Daddy."

"Diane…your Mom, would kill me if I let you." I knew he was right. Dad was the breadwinner. Mom was the boss of health and safety.

"Okay, Dad. Today, okay, but after today I think I can do it." All he said in reply was, "We'll see." He was playing it smart. It really wasn't his decision or mine. Mom would let us know when it was okay.

I got up and got dressed. I put little effort into it. Just threw on my bra, panties, t-shirt, track pants and a baggy t-shirt. Hair in a pony. Baseball cap. No make-up. I ate a protein bar for breakfast. I didn't even know what time was my appointment was. I just let my parents take over all the specifics. It was a relief, but something I knew I couldn't and they wouldn't let go on for long. Around 10 am, my Dad informed me it was time to go.

Walking into the counselor's office, I caught my reflection in the mirror on the way up the stairs to the second floor. *Who was that?* She looked something like me, but tired, washed out. I had never seen myself so pale and devoid of expression. It was not the me I knew or identified with. I looked on the outside like I felt on the inside. Now there was no denying to anyone that I wasn't okay.

No one told me if the counselor I was going to see was male or female. I was a little surprised when the sign on the door read, Matthew White, PhD, Clinical Psychologist. I wondered if he would be like my Dad, in his early fifties, or much younger. Maybe I didn't want to talk to a guy. I mean, that was my problem, right? Guys? But telling someone like my Mom might be worse. A Mom would be ashamed of me.

I stepped up to the sliding window at the reception desk and knocked lightly. A receptionist slid it open.

"I'm...uh...Biz...Elizabeth Connelly. I have an appointment." I informed her.

"Yes, Elizabeth....Would you prefer I call you Biz?" I nodded yes. "Your appointment is in a few minutes. Here are some forms to fill out. Then just take them in when Dr. Matt comes to get you."

There wasn't anyone else in the waiting room except my Dad. I really liked that. I was still feeling pretty shaky. It was concerning. Was I losing my mind? What exactly was wrong with me?

The door by the sliding glass window opened and a medium build light brown-haired man in his mid-thirties walked out. "Biz?" he asked looking at me. My Dad stood up when I did. The man introduced himself to both of us.

"I'm Dr. White. Most of my patients call me Dr. Matt, though. Ready to begin, Biz?"

My Dad moved to go with me.

I put my hand up. "I got it, Dad, it's okay." Dr. Matt smiled and nodded at my Dad, like it was a good thing. Dad sat back down.

My session with Dr. Matt was fifty minutes long and I swear I cried through the whole thing. I didn't want to cry and I was even mad at myself for doing so. He stuck with me the whole time as I heaved and gulped out my story. How I let myself be used and even invited more abuse once I already felt so very bad about myself. How I hadn't and still didn't expect to be treated poorly by people, especially ones I thought cared for me. How I cut myself off and tried to kill all my feelings with alcohol and "the other poor choices." Hell, I couldn't even articulate it, the slutty sex, I was so ashamed. Dr. Matt listened. He took notes and handed me tissues. I'm fairly certain his trash can was going to have to be emptied right after the session, I'd filled it up so much. Toward the end, he told me he thought I was having post-traumatic stress. I frowned and challenged him. I hadn't been to war or anything, so how was that possible? He told me how stress affects different people in different ways. My stress came from trauma over broken trust-something I'd never experienced to that extent before. I was also having symptoms of panic. He wanted to see me every day one-on-one for a while and then after a week I could go to a group for stress and anxiety, too. He also called my regular doctor to prescribe some anti-anxiety medication. I cried over all of that, too. I knew I was crazy. Dr. Matt assured me I wasn't.

I didn't drive to see Dr. Matt the next day or for the whole next week. My Dad or Mom drove me. They hovered and babied, but never asked for answers. I cried and talked and cried with Dr. Matt. We discussed why it hurt so bad. Why I made bad decisions. Steps, little ones to take each day to feel better. I took the anti-anxiety medicine when I felt like I would shake apart from panic. Like I was going to die. I didn't want to die. I just thought I might. Dr. Matt taught me when I panicked to tell myself it would be over in 5 minutes. He also taught me my mantra.

After a week of almost constant supervision and chauffeuring, I was feeling like it was time to try a bit on my own. Admittedly, I wasn't 100 percent and I even felt unsure about trying, but I decided to give it a go. I got up without being awoken, showered, dried my hair with the blow dryer (something I don't think I'd done in a month), even put on make-up. Entering the kitchen for breakfast, the look on my parents' faces was my reward for being a little brave. They both smiled. Closed lip smiles, all the way up to their eyes.

"Oh, sweetie, you look so nice…so much better," my Mom said emotionally. Dad just continued to smile and shook his head in agreement.

"I'm going to drive myself, today and every day after. Treatment group starts soon and that takes longer. You don't need to sit around and wait for me this way."

My Dad cleared his throat, "I wouldn't have cared if I had to sit for eight hours a day. I am just so happy to see a bit of my Biz kid back." I kissed him on the head for that one. I'm 21, but he's still my Daddy.

I worked my treatment program as best I could. I knew I had about seven weeks to pull it together before I needed to go back to school. My parents asked me once, only once, if I still wanted to go to Weldon. They were giving me an out. I could have taken it, but I told them, Yes, I was determined to finish my degree at Weldon. Something about not going back and facing down all the perceptions of me from last year felt cowardly. Getting better meant being brave. I took to heart everything Dr. Matt worked through with me. I had been hurt. My trust had been broken. I didn't trust myself. I tried to punish myself. Panic was my fight-or-flight reaction. I had been traumatized. And I wasn't alone. Many people panic. Many people suffer from PTSD. I was just facing it. By the time I was a week away from going back to school I didn't need my anti-anxiety meds anymore. I was only taking them when I felt a panic attack coming on. They were getting less and less with the use of other strategies. Oh, I still had the pills, in case I needed them. I wasn't brave enough to go back without them, but it felt good to need them less.

The day before I left to go back to Weldon, I met with Dr. Matt.

"What do you think about going back, Biz?" he asked candidly.

I replied, "I'd be lying if I said I wasn't nervous. I feel unsure. I don't feel like the same person I was before all of this. I feel a little beat up, but a little smarter too. I don't feel as 'light' as I used to. Do you know what I mean?" He shook his head yes. "It's harder to be open, to joke. I am a more careful Biz now."

"I rarely give advice, Biz, I try just to listen and coach, but I'm going to break my rule a little. My thought is, don't be too careful. Don't hide your light under a bushel. Don't forget Biz. The Real Biz.

Not this summer's Biz. You will eventually be able to trust again. Yourself and others."

Armed with his words and my determination, my mantra and my just-in-case Xanax, I packed up and took myself back to Weldon for senior year.

Chapter 16: NOW-January

Winter break over, I am back at Weldon. I did a lot of thinking while away. I only cried or moped when I was alone in my room or out of the house and talking or texting Jules. As far as I could tell, my parents appeared unconcerned. They didn't baby me or look worried like they did every time I was around them last summer. I had a few sessions with Dr. Matt. We talked through my year so far. He reminded me of his advice-to not be too careful. To not lose "Biz." We discussed what a balancing act that was. I went out with a few of my high school friends and had drinks a couple of times. I even went to a New Year's Eve party at my wealthy friend, Shari's big house. I danced and socialized with old friends, but did not drink too much and did NOT kiss anyone at midnight. My mind was already a whirl of feelings and emotions. Why add something stupid and meaningless to it? I was trying to not lose "Biz," and stay even. The balancing act.

Classes start back on Monday. I am here the Wednesday before. RAs can get back in the dorms a few days earlier than regular students to get things ready. There will be some changes in rooms after people decide they no longer like their original roommate. Maintenance inspections, stuff like that. The rest of the students will filter back in between Friday and Sunday. I have seen most of the other RAs, except Suzette. I am constantly on the lookout for her, but always relieved when I don't see her. In my time away I have decided to reserve my judgment. Maybe I am fabricating my suspicions about Jake and Suzette. I mean, aren't I just as bad? I had been hanging out with Davis a lot. I hug him all the time. And call him names. And…he kissed me, like REALLY kissed me. I admitted to myself I wanted him. During my time away, I sent a text to Davis.

Please call or text me.

He texted me back.

Not yet, Biz

I was sad and I admit, I cried a bit when I read it. *He's not going to talk to me again. He's not going to touch me again. God, I miss him. That's it, I miss him. I miss my friend. I miss my friend that I kissed in a not-friend way.*

The day before I was to leave to go back to school, Jake texted me.

How's your break going? Are you having fun? I need to talk to you when you get back.

I responded flippantly.

Break has been great. Having fun with my HS friends. Sure, let's talk.

I didn't know quite what to think of his text, but I knew what mine meant. I was willing to listen. I wanted an explanation. I wanted to know exactly what was going on. I wanted to know why he thought I was sleeping with Davis. Was Jake with *me*? Was he with *Suzette*? Davis once told me that after the first party, Jake had said, "Biz is a girl I could fall in love with." When Davis told me that I was ecstatic. I had believed my relationship with Jake could be something. Something that wouldn't sweep me away. A relationship I could control. I wouldn't be the naïve girl I was last year with Neil. It was going to be possible to have an honest relationship. A mature relationship; one that wasn't about being with each other all the time. Allowing space for the other person to do what they needed to do, but coming together at the end of the time apart. It didn't have to be all-consuming and I didn't have to give up my sense of self. Someone I could trust to love me. I was also coming to realize that I wasn't defined by Jake. I would be okay if he didn't want to be with me. More than not being with him, I was afraid of repeating the public rejection and humiliation of last year and not being in control. I had been holding back to be careful. But was what I was pursuing with Jake really a relationship, really love? I was very involved with Davis, whether I admitted it or not. With Davis, I was "Biz." With Jake, I was careful. Really, neither one of them was "mine," in any sustainable way.

I made my decision. I could be with neither. But I wanted to let them know on my terms. I wasn't going to let Jake have the satisfaction of breaking up with me. I couldn't stay in the "friend zone," with Davis and watch him be with Kathleen. It all had to change.

My opportunity came sooner than I had expected. It's the Friday before the start of Spring Semester and I am eating dinner in the cafeteria with Jules and Charlie. There are a few other early-semester arrivers here and some of the other RAs. Midway through my meal, I sense someone approaching me on my left through the cafeteria doors. Turning slightly, Jake, holding Suzette's hand, comes into view. I am having déjà vu from last spring. Neil. Robyn. The cafeteria. The humiliation. I hear Jules' inhale. My first thought is PANIC. Run. Then I feel an overwhelming sense of knowing what to do. I've made my decisions and I'm ready. Jake approaches. I stand and face him. He has a yellow tinge around his left eye, like an old bruise. *What's that?* It throws me off for a second. But just a second. Jake opens his mouth to talk and I cut him off.

"Oh, no, I am not doing this here! Follow me." I motion back toward the cafeteria entrance. He does, as I march out of the cafeteria. I hiss at him, "Just you, no Suzette." *I CAN DO THIS.* As we walk out, I think I hear someone call my name.

***

Jake is behind me. He is actually a little beside me and behind me, but I am walking fast. I told him to leave Suzette in the cafeteria and he did. Internally, I am smiling at the guts it took me to do so.

We walk up the stairs with Jake chattering in my ear, "Jeez, Biz. Slow

down. Just stop for a second. We don't have to run all over the

dorms. Let's just stop. I need to talk to you."

"I know. That's what you said in your text." I don't exactly

know what's going to come out of my mouth. I walk us to the south

turret room on the second floor of Lawrence Hall, where I had so

many Game Nights with Jake and Suzette. He scoots in front of me

and turns on me.

"What is it Biz? What is so important that you had to drag me

all the way up here?" I am just about to open my mouth, to say what?

That I forgive him or that I'm done? I don't know. The "failure is not

an option" part of me wants to tell him I'm sorry I was acting so weird

before break and to please forgive me. No, I've made the decision. I

need to end things.

Jake shifts his eyes off of my face and over my shoulder.

"Davis?"

Davis is here? Davis is here. What the hell is Davis doing

here? Davis is HERE! I am going to see him!

These are my exact thoughts before I whip around to see his face. Davis' face, his penetrating green eyes. I am a bit mad, but mostly relieved, and honestly... beyond excited to see him. Davis looks upset and working really hard to hold it together.

"Davis. . . I"

"Biz. . . come with me."

"I'm talking to Jake ab. . ."

He cuts me off. "Come. With. Me… right now, Biz!" He sniffs and looks right at Jake. Jake seems to cower. Davis lowers his voice and speaks over my shoulder to Jake, " Jake, she needs to come with me. You can stay here and wait or go to your room or wherever it is you go." Davis voice drips with sarcasm on the last option he mentions. "I'll bring her back to you when I'm done."

"When you're done?" I turn on Davis and snap out with a bit of a shriek. "No way am I going anywhere with you."

"Stop it, Biz. Just come on." He grabs my elbow firmly and walks me down the hall to the ancient Disco elevator. I suddenly realize that Jake said nothing-Not. One. Thing.-when Davis arrived and took me. Davis is angry, or maybe not angry, determined. I've never really seen this much emotion from him. He is generally so cool

170

and calm. Something has him really worked up. It's getting me worked up. It is, dare I say it, hot. He pushes the button to call the elevator and miraculously it arrives immediately. That never happens. Still clutching my elbow with his other hand, he shoves the outer elevator door and then the gate right afterward open. It is effortless for him. It would take both my hands and all my strength to get it open, so now I know he's agitated. He drags me in and punches the button for the fifth floor. My dorm room is on the fifth floor. Is that where we are going? I am getting a little scared by his behavior, but mostly I am curious. The elevator is small. It is hard to fit more than three people in it. Davis is so... something right now... something that makes it feels like he is taking up more than his usual amount of space. He turns on me and pins me to the wall by putting a hand on each side of it by my head. He leans his face in very close. He is breathing really heavily. I can feel it on my face. I close my eyes for a second and realize... I have missed being near him. I can smell him and I've missed that smell. . . that Davis smell, clean, but sweaty and warm. After a few moments, I open my eyes. Davis is still right in front of me. "I just couldn't let you stay there with him and get destroyed," he says huskily.

"So, you decided to play white knight and save me?" I question. "Because, I think I had it under control. I didn't really know what I was going to say, but I figured I'd hear him out. Wait? Why did you think I'd get destroyed?" He moves away a bit. The elevator stops after its excruciatingly slow ascent to five. We stand there and stare at the doors, both realizing they are not going to open unless one of us opens them. Davis sighs heavily and takes my hand, entwining his fingers in mine. I don't pull away. I like it. Again, he throws open the doors of the elevator like it's a patio door. He pulls me the three doors down to my dorm room and motions at it with his other hand. I pull the key out of my jeans and open the door. He releases my hand, and escorts me into the room by putting his hand on the small of my back. Davis has touched me before, hugged me, so why does this feel so new and different. He slightly lifts me and sets me gently on my elevated loft bed. With him standing and me sitting, we are eye to eye. "I didn't want to be the one to tell you this, Biz. I didn't want to be the one to hurt you. But you are just so damn naïve and trusting. The thing is….when I got back from break, Charlie invited me to a band practice to see if I had any suggestions for their sound. I was trying to avoid Jake, but while I was there, I overheard him talking. We'd already had, how do I say this, WORDS before break, after he accused you of sleeping with me. I heard him talking about when he saw your picture, the one of you and Charlie that Smitty took when you went on the road trip. The one of you and Charlie hugging in a crazy way. The one I said I saw and that's how I recognized you that first day in the cafeteria. He said that when he saw that picture in Charlie's room and then heard the story about what happened to you last year, he realized you were the girl that was 'banging his RA, Neil.' He said he'd hear you guys having sex from all the way down the hall. I was furious listening to him talk about how you were probably SO vulnerable now and how 'he knew he just had to get some of that' chick. He started going off about how you were so sweet and just the kind of girl that would always stay with him, but that you just wouldn't 'give it up,' so when Suzette came along the night of the kegger it was all so easy... Then he continued to brag, 'Biz didn't suspect a thing. She was probably too busy with Davis. She called and texted me like a million times when I was with Suzette right before break. When Suzette asked me about them, I told Suz it served Biz right for doing Davis.' Fucking hypocrite."

173

My eyes start to well up. Davis looks at me, concerned that I am going to cry. What he doesn't know is that I cry at just about everything. I cry when I am sad. But I REALLY cry when I am angry, which I am. I also cry when I am happy. Right now, even with all my anger toward Jake, I am happy. Happy because although he hasn't said in specific words and I am just coming to realize it, I can tell Davis cares about me. And I care about him. Even if all we will ever be is friends.

"I am going to kill him!" I scream. "He knew, he knew about Neil and all of that," I jump off the loft bed, practically falling into Davis' arms.

"Oh, no you're not, Dragon!" He stops me with a chuckle.

"Dragon?"

"Yes, a dragon is a bigger, badder version of a Lizard. And also, because you are breathing fire right now." I roll my eyes to the ceiling, not believing I am laughing in the middle of this conversation. "Yeah, that's what I called you, so what? Biz, listen to me. You're not going to run down there like a crazy person or run away. Here is what you are going to do."

Davis talks to me about what he thought Jake was about to do. Break up with me publicly and painfully, like Neil. I let Davis know I'm not mad at him for telling me what he heard. I was already beginning to suspect Jake wasn't what he seemed. It was just easier, in my mind, to try and see the best in Jake. To not think he could be anything like Neil. Davis and I went through everything again about last year's confrontation with Neil and Robyn in the cafeteria and why I was so torn up about it. And the guys. All the random guys afterward. How it wasn't my fault. How I had been played in the cruelest way possible, just for the sport of it, by Neil, and now by Jake. How I had little control over what happened, because I was a trusting person and I was hurting. How I had wanted to hurt myself. How Jake's intentions didn't match his actions, at least not his behaviors at the beginning. He started out acting so sensitive and solicitous, but he couldn't maintain it and the truth was leaking out. I told Davis the decisions I made over break about Jake. I had planned to hear him out, but still guard my heart. I left out the part about how I intended things to end with Davis, too. I needed to control the finish of this thing with Jake first. In all of the romantic "relationships" I'd ever had, I'd never had any say in the outcome. They hadn't been honest and truthful. It takes about two hours, but Davis and I come up with a plan.

***

Deep breaths. *I can do this. I CAN SO TOTALLY DO this.* On an average day, I repeat this phrase to myself often, but today, right now, marching down the stairs from the fifth floor to the second floor, I actually believe it. Believe it deep down. Davis is trailing behind me. I have asked him to come, but told him to stay at a Minimum Safe Distance. That made him laugh. He is hanging back, down the hall and slightly around the corner from Jake's door.

One more deep breath. I can hear some talking inside. I knock with purpose. Jake answers and as he pulls the door further open, I can see Suzette. She doesn't look happy. But not because I'm there. I think she was already unhappy.

"Jake, I want to say something and then I'm going to leave."

"Biz, no… let's talk about this."

I continue, not acknowledging his plea. "You're a damn hypocrite. I was never with Davis like that. You were just looking for a way to keep me and bang Suzette at the same time. I don't want a scene and I don't want any drama. I want you to know that I really thought you were a great guy, even when you weren't. I wanted so badly to be your girlfriend. For you to really know me, love me. I don't think you know how to do that. I don't know if I do either, but I am pretty sure you are not the person I am supposed to figure that out with. I know what you did," I gesture to Suzette. "I sort of get why, but it was really shitty of you. And I don't want to be with you anymore."

"C'mon, Biz," he pleads.

"Why are you even saying that, Jake? You don't want me. You want to use me. You're probably using Suzette. Goodbye, Jake… Remember, No Drama. I don't want to hear about this in the cafeteria and all over Weldon until I graduate. And another thing…" I am just guessing here, but given the look of his face I say it. "I'm glad Davis punched you. Then I add, "Oh, and Suzette, I am NOT sorry I barfed on your stupid one-of-a-kind furry Ugg slippers."

He shuts the door and immediately I hear Suzette yelling.

"Oh My God. . . .She broke up with you! That is hilarious! After you were kicking me to the curb, she broke up with you." Shaking my head, I turn and walk away. When I finally look up, there is Davis at the end of the hall.

Chapter 17: NOW-After the Break-up

I slowly walk down to Davis, looking into his mischievous eyes. They're laughing. "I heard the whole thing. . .you were amazing, Biz." I pick up speed as I close the distance and run straight into his arms. He hugs me tight and swings me around, "You did it!" I melt into his chest, sighing and then inhaling his scent. I love that smell. I could just stay like this forever. *Whoa, I COULD just stand here like this forever.* He pulls away, tips my head up by my chin and gently rubs his hand along my jaw. I think my heart will jump out of my chest. The zap and buzz I feel when I am around him is going crazy. Stronger than ever. He pulls away, smiles and then turns slightly, as if to leave.

I reach out for his hand, lacing our fingers together. "Where are you going?"

He tilts his head slightly, "Back to my place. I just came by to make sure you didn't get hurt. I'm glad I could help." He sounds down.

"Not so fast, Mister."

"Mister?"

"What, like that's worse than being called a Dragon?"

Davis looks amused and allows me to lead him back to the Disco elevator and press the up button. "Are we really going up in that thing again?" he complains mildly, gesturing to the elevator door.

"Davis, it's been a rough day. Second semester hasn't even started yet. I don't have the energy to climb the stairs one more time, so once it gets here, whip open that door again and then walk me back to my room... Mister." The elevator is taking a little longer than usual. It's so unpredictable. Standing in front of it waiting, I look down at our hands together. Then I turn my head slightly and look all the way up him. Physically, he is remarkably stunning. I knew Davis had a beautiful body, ever since the night he slept on my floor, but have never allowed myself to think about it for very long. I eventually get to his eyes. My favorite thing about him. So far. He's been watching me watch him and gives be a half grin. We fuse into each other—looking at one another in a way we never did or could before.

The elevator's arrival is announced with a ding that pulls us out of our mutual daze. We get in and Davis quickly shuts the gate and door. It's a small elevator. Even with just the two of us, there isn't room to pace or move really.

Davis asks softly, "Are you really okay?"

"Yeah, I think I am" And I really do think I am, but now I have to figure out how the heck I am going to talk about my feelings, my decision about Davis. "Mavis?...."

"Aw, Jeez are you gonna start that again?"

I giggle. "Maybe." Then I become serious. "Why did you come help me?" He sighs a really long sigh and hits the emergency stop button on the elevator. The ancient lift bumps to a halt. The small space is now buzzing with energy. My hairs on my arms are standing up and my heart is beating a little faster.

180

"What you had or what you thought you were going to have with Jake was not love. It wasn't anything like love." *Okay, here comes the lecture from Mr. Engaged Dude.* He turns away slightly and runs his hand through his hair. I would love to reach up and touch it. It's only then that I notice it looks different, shorter. He's cut his hair like in that dream I had. He's wearing a black fitted button down, too. Just like in the dream. *I hope this isn't just a dream.* Turning back to me he says, "I know what love looks like." *I am going to puke if he starts talking about his girlfriend and I'm more than a little jealous.* "I was…" He turns on me. "NO, I AM in love…" He is right in my face, his forehead almost on mine. We are still holding hands. Man, am I confused. All I can think to say is *Lucky Girl*, so I do. Sadly.

"Lucky Girl."

Davis' amazing green eyes lock onto mine and I see them go from very serious to crinkling up with amusement.

"I hope SHE thinks so." In the next second, he kisses me quickly. I can't think to do anything but respond and I kiss him back, lots of small kisses, that soon turn to a slow, deep kiss that I am wishing would never stop. My heart is pounding so loudly, surely

Davis can hear it. During the kiss I have thrown my arms around his neck and have my hands in the back of his hair. *It feels so thick and silky. . .I've always wondered how it felt.* He has one hand on the back of my neck and one on the small of my back, urging me forward toward his pelvis while at the same time pushing up against the carpeted wall of the Disco elevator. *Wait. This guy is engaged. Shit, Biz. Knock it off.* That thought prompts me to pull away from his lips. I bring my hands to Davis' chest and push away. He is not letting me move from him and has moved on to kissing the side of my mouth and my cheeks and eyes. I grab both sides of his jaw with both of my hands to stop him and look him in the eyes.

He softly and sexily whispers to me, "Because SHE is YOU."

I am very surprised, confused but surprised and well, relieved. My eyes begin to well up. My head is spinning from the past few hours and this is pushing me over the edge. I give out a little sob. "I thought. . . I thought you were talking about your fiancée?"

"No, Lizard Breath, YOU." Tears fall down my face and I am laughing and crying at the same time. Only Davis would say something so sweet and tease me by calling be that nickname at the same time. He is laughing, too, and his eyes are a bit glazed over.

182

"Just you. As a matter of fact, that's why I ran off so quickly when I kissed you after finding you crying in The Space. It was hell to stay away from you, but I couldn't be with you until…..Biz, I broke up with Kathleen."

"Really?"

"Really. I didn't know how this would all work out, but I needed to be better for you. Better than Jake, than anyone. After you kissed me, I needed to make it right. I decided NOT to wait. To do something right away to change how things were going. That's why I left you so suddenly. I am going way out on a limb with this…risking a lot. I think you probably deserve better than me, but I know that's not Neil or Jake or any of those idiots that hurt you. If you'll let me, I'd like to prove it to you." I'm unsure if I get all the words he says after he calls me Lizard Breath, because my head is spinning with joy. I get the gist, really I do, and they are wonderful words to hear. I'm sure subconsciously, I'm absorbing them all and will replay them over and over in the future, but in this moment all I think to say is, "Mavis." Then I pretty much just fling myself at him. He pushes the entire length of his body up against mine and I push right back. My nipples are instantly tight. I feel my body shivering at the same time the

183

space between my legs is beginning to feel very warm. And we kiss. I suck on his bottom lip as his tongue parts mine and strokes my tongue. I have never kissed so long and hard in my life, barely stopping to breath before slamming our lips and tongues into each other again.

Davis pulls the emergency stop button and the elevator starts moving. After what seems like minutes more of holding each other and kissing, the elevator dings to a stop on the fifth floor. Davis puts both hands low under my butt and hikes me up so my thighs wrap around his waist and I am positioned right...there. All the while he is still kissing me. He reaches over and once again throws open the gate and door to the elevator. Still kissing me and holding me firmly against him, he walks out of the elevator and down the short distance to my dorm room.

I hear a few people down the hall whisper, none too quietly, "Holy crap, is that Biz? Who is she with? I don't think it's Jake." I couldn't care less. Davis slides my body down his when we get to my door, allowing me to feel every inch of him.

"Biz, you're here," Davis informs me, still looking deeply into my eyes. I'm whimpering at the loss of contact. I don't want to stop kissing him. I don't want him to stop holding me against ALL of him.

"You wanted me to walk you back to your room, right?" I can't speak. Davis loves me. He shifts his gaze repeatedly toward something to the side of me. Oh, he's indicating my door. "Lizard Breath, you need to get your key out." He laughs at me, amused at my silence.

"Oh, right." I finally answer. I get it out, unlock the door and walk through, still holding Davis' hand. He doesn't move through the door with me so I turn around, "Mavis?"

"You do know calling me that is sort of emasculating, right?"

"Trust me, nothing could emasculate you," I tease as I tug him into my room. "Please come in."

"Are you sure about this?" he asks gently. I nod yes. "Because if we do this, it won't be a one time thing. You are going to be stuck with me."

"Yes, I'm sure."

Standing in the middle of my room, he pulls me close. He kisses my hair on the top of my head, and then moves to my forehead. I tip my face up to take in his gorgeous dark green eyes and they are full of love and...lust.

"I've missed you so much, Biz." He kisses every part of my face and is turning his attention to the area below my ear and down my neck. I grasp his shoulders and slide my hands down his thick muscular arms and then back up to clench them around his neck and run my fingers up into his hair again. As this is happening, I can't shut up. I just keep talking, rapidly and excitedly, "Davis…Oh, I've missed you, too," I gasp. "Mav, I can't believe this is happening… I am so happy. Baby, I have wanted you so much. I dreamed of you. I dreamed of you, just like this. Shorter hair, black shirt. Is this a dream? Oh, I hope this is not a dream." *I cannot shut up.* Davis has run his hands down my back and up under my t-shirt in front. One of his hands has come up to cup my breast. He runs his thumb over one of my tight, aching nipples. Lower down, I feel the unreal vibration and heat intensify. "That feels amazing…" I tell him.

"You are doing that babbling thing again, Lizard," Davis moans near my mouth as I begin to move my hands down to his lower back to where his jeans begin.

"I know, I'm sorry, I get excited." I gasp.

I hear a smile in his voice. "I can tell. I have to tell you when you do that… that babbling thing? It turns me on so much. Every

186

time you do it, I think about how excited you are. How you'd sound if I made love to you. The excited noises you'd make when I was inside you. It gets to me, everywhere." He pulls me up to him, slightly tilting his hips. I look down. He is excited. Hard. Ready.

"I don't know how to stop talking so much. You might have to help me." And with that phrase his mouth is slashed to mine. Licking underneath my top lip, biting the bottom, and then violently both our lips part and our tongues are tangled in each other. I moan loudly. Clothes are flying off at light speed. We stop kissing only long enough so that both our shirts come up and over our heads and are tossed in a pile at the end of the bed. Davis steps back and looks at me and lets out a long sigh.

"What's wrong?" I frown.

He is staring at my pale pink bra with black ribbon trim. "Nothing anymore."

Pulling me in to kiss me again, his hands sweep around my back and he unfastens my bra, slides it off my arms and throws it into the pile with the shirt. The feeling of his beautiful, ridged chest and abs against me sends a burning sensation right down to my toes. I am doing everything to savor the moment and not just throw myself on him and wrap my legs around his waist. Davis has other ideas. He has leaned down and cupping my breast, laves the tightened nipple with his tongue, and he then sucks it into his lips, licking it hard with his tongue. The burning sensation increases rapidly.

"Please, please, I want you so badly. Mmmmm. Please."

"We'll get there, Lizard. Trust me."

"I do." I realize right then, I do trust him. Completely. It only amps up my need.

Davis kisses down my body and circles his tongue in my belly button. I giggle. He stops briefly, looks up and smiles at me with those gorgeous guy-linered eyes. Then he's right back at it. Unbuttoning my jeans, he pushes them over my hips. As he slides them down my legs, his nose is rubbing up and down the front of my matching panties.

"You smell so sweet and hot." His voice is husky. Davis inhales deeply and kisses me over the top of my panties at the apex of my thighs...right... there. Soft, erotic, tingly kisses. I slide my hands across his strong muscular shoulders and then up into his hair. So soft. And then, suddenly, in a series of fast, urgent moves, he stands. My hands fly to his jeans and rip at the buttons. Grasping my lower back and pulling me to him, while I push his jeans downward, with the other hand he gives them a shove so they move lower and kicks them off and grabs them with a free hand at the same time. He lays them over the edge of the bed.

Turning back to me, he whispers, "Hi."

"Hi, back, Baby." I say.

"Baby." Davis growls. He puts his hands on my hips by my panties and in a swift move, glides them quickly down my legs. I step out and push my completely naked body against him. The fabric of his black boxer briefs rubs deliciously against the bundle of nerves firing out of control between my legs.

"No Stewie boxers?"

"Not tonight, Baby, and no Stewie imitations either."

Davis scoops me up and lies me on my elevated bed. Then crawls up my body from the bottom of the bed.

"I want you, Biz, so much." I reach up and feel his erection through his boxer briefs. I stroke it firmly upward with one hand and pull him down to me with the other. Putting my hand in the back of his boxers, I assist him in removing them. When I look at him, naked, over me, I shiver. He is beautiful, long and powerful. And I made

189

him that way. I've never felt powerful with a man before. It makes me unbelievably hot.

Reaching between my legs, Davis circles his thumb at the apex. I close my eyes and absorb the build up. I am close already. Keeping his thumb on my clit and pushing a finger into me and circling, Davis groans, "You are SO ready." When I open my eyes, his eyes are burning into me. He is still touching me down there, but I notice he has a condom on.

"When did you?" I question.

"I have hidden talents," he looks down at himself, "...and not so hidden talents."

I can't stand it any longer. I push up on one elbow and pull him onto me. I pump my pelvis over his erection. He slides over my cleft and with a thrust is inside. Filling me. Hot and pulsing.

"Oh, my god, Lizard, Baby. You feel so amazing."

"Please move, Mavis. Baby, please."

"Just a second...okay, okay."

He rocks into me deeply. Holding me by the nape of my neck with one hand, he places his thumb over my clit and circles while pushing down slightly, every now and then lowering his lips to soulfully take my mouth. We move in a deep, driving rhythm. I feel myself clenching down on him. Slowly, steadily tensing. I am so close. The sensation is overwhelming. As I fall violently into the crushing orgasm, all I can do is mouth almost voicelessly, "Oh, Oh, Ohhhhhh." Davis is not far behind me, I feel his whole body stiffen and shudder, as he calls my name.

My real name.

Chapter 18: NOW-Hiding out

I wake up again to the sunlight streaming in my window and stare at the wall. But this time, I know it's my wall. And I know it's Davis' arms I am lying in naked, my back to his chest. I am completely relaxed and content. Sighing, I replay our evening in my head.

I feel his warm breath on my neck. I shift to move and he pulls me back toward him and kisses my shoulder.

"I thought you were still asleep."

"No, I've been awake for a little while. Just holding you, thinking of the best way to wake you up."

"What did you decide?"

"I've been going back and forth between a few things. At first, I was thinking coffee, but now I think, maybe…"

He slips down under the duvet and kisses down my back. I feel him slide his hand to my waist and then lower it to my knee. Flipping me toward him, he pushes my knee to the side. I feel his mouth on the inner part of my lower thigh. He begins to deliver a series of slow, soft kisses and a few licks all the way up until he gets to the apex of my legs.

"This," I hear him say under the covers.

I push the duvet back so I can see him. As I do, I see his head dip down to lick my already achy clit. It takes no time at all for him to arouse me. Just kissing down my back. Or maybe, I was already ready when I awoke.

Davis licks with light delicate strokes and then circles the tip of his tongue over the top, under the hood. It completely unhinges me. My fingers are in his hair and my pelvis is rotating, begging silently for more. A few deep suckles and a some quick flicking of his talented tongue and I come hard, saying "Davis, god." Wave after wave of clenching spasms.

He kneels back quickly onto his heels and reaches into his jeans lying across the bed post behind him, pulling a condom packet from his jeans. Aaah, that's where it came from last night. I wonder how many he has? He hands it to me and I tear it open with my teeth and roll it onto his readiness. Davis yanks me up hard, so I am straddling his upright kneeling body and positions me over his rigid penis.

"Take me, Lizard. I love you, take me."

I slide my already throbbing self down onto him with a groan. I want him. I want to show him I love him. I ride him hard, sliding up and then pushing down. I rock hard to get him as far inside me as possible. My clit is rubbing against where our bodies meet and the intensity builds quickly. He is grabbing my hips, directing the motion and depth. Suddenly he wraps his arms around my body, pulling me close as he releases into me with a long, powerful moan. With that, I go over the edge again.

We are still naked and wrapped around each other in bed an hour later. My stomach complains loudly.

Davis chuckles and, putting his hand flat on my belly says, "I think we need to feed you."

"I don't want to leave this room. I just want to stay with you all day, like this."

"Exactly like this?" he asks. I nod in the affirmative.

"We are going to have to get up eventually, but for now, how about I throw on my clothes and go get us some coffee and something to eat. You stay here." He is so sweet. Coffee in bed.

***

When Davis returns, I am sitting up in bed against the headboard. I have put on a black tank top and retrieved some panties from my drawer. I am grinning like an idiot when the door opens and beautiful, sexy Davis is standing there with two coffees and a bag of something that smells incredible.

"Delivery boy!" He jokes.

"You certainly are," I joke back, and wave both hands toward myself frantically to indicate I would like my coffee… and him…to be delivered to me immediately.

Davis takes off his jeans and shirt and returns to bed. "Now we can stay here all day."

Sitting in bed, next to each other sipping our coffee and eating our chocolate croissants, *(Good call, Mavis)* I describe to him the decisions I made on winter break. First, the decision to confront Jake and offer him the chance to try again or just be friends. Davis tells me I was being over-generous. I agree, but know I will always choose to trust. We concur that it doesn't matter. Not now. Jake is history. I proceed to tell Davis how I was prepared to give him up, too.

"Really, you were just going to walk away?"

"It was a hard decision. I was dreading talking to you. But I would have done it, to do the right thing. You are my friend. My best friend. It would have hurt for a long, long time. But I knew I couldn't be just friends. I trust you more than anyone. I couldn't be with you if you belonged to someone else. I would never do that to another person. Because I love you." Tears are building up at the back of my eyes. "I love you so much."

"I've been waiting for you to say that. Wondering if you would. It sounds better than I imagined," he says, his voice full of emotion.

We kiss. Not the frenzied passionate kisses of last night and this morning. Sweet, loving kisses.

In between kisses, he tells me in a low voice, "Not only do I love you, Biz, I happen to like you. I was not going to get into any of

196

this with you with any guilt. I was not about to make you the 'other woman,' and you deserve better than a cheater."

"That's exactly how I felt," I reply.

"I'm so glad you didn't have to make that decision. I'm yours, Lizard. Just you. And you're mine. I'm the one who stays."

We do just what we planned and stay in the room all day. In bed, talking and cuddling and making love. Slow, gentle love. Many times. When I next look at the clock it's 6 pm. All I've had on all day, at the most, are a tank top and panties. As I ponder how it will feel to walk out into the world as Davis' girl, a knock comes to the door.

"Biz, we know you are in there, so just open up. Come on. You haven't been answering your texts." It's Jules. I can tell by the voice. I giggle and look at Davis' naked body in my bed and wink at him.

"She's not going to go away. You'd better cover up," I tell him. I grab his jeans off the end of my bed and throw them at him.

Facing the door and pulling on my panties and Davis' black shirt, I yell, "Coming."

This only makes Davis chuckle loudly. I go to the door, take a deep breath and open it a crack. It's Jules, but she's not alone.

"Hi, Jules… Charlie."

"Everything okay? Last I saw you, you were blazing out of the cafeteria with Jake behind you and then Davis came in and ran after both of you. I thought I would have heard from you by now." Jules says with concern.

"It's all good…really good." I am pretty sure I am smirking and blushing. I rub one of my feet against my leg.

"So, everything straightened out with Jake?" she whispers.

"We broke up…I guess…since I don't know if we ever really were anything."

Jules is standing in my doorway looking very confused. She looks up at Charlie, who shrugs his shoulders and then points into my room. "So, who?"

I feel Davis' arm slip around my waist and Jules' eyes go to it. Then I feel his naked chest against my back, his pelvis pushed into my bottom. He peeks his head over my shoulder and with his free hand opens the door wider to reveal us both in our half-dressed, mussed up hair state to Jules and Charlie.

Davis says, "She's with me." The way he says it is full of meaning. Simultaneously announcing that he is with me now, but also claiming me for the future, publicly to my friends. It feels incredible. I turn my head to kiss him right on the mouth.

I confirm right before I kiss him, "Mmmm, I am."

Jules is momentarily speechless, opening and closing her mouth a few times like a goldfish and then stating, "Well, Thank god….. I told you, you'd make a hot couple."

Davis smiles and asks me, "She did?"

"Yes."

"And what did you say?"

"At the time, I blew it off because you were taken."

"What do you say now?"

"Yes," I giggle. "We are a hot couple."

"Damn right we are."

Davis begins kissing behind my ear and down my neck, while closing the door on Jules and Charlie. Charlie brings his hand out to stop the closure, warning Davis, "Dude, you better not hurt her. I am serious."

Davis stops kissing me, looks me right in the eyes, then turns his face to Charlie and tells him with full sincerity, "That's the last thing I have in mind for this little Lizard. Bye, Charlie." Charlie removes his hand with a smile and winks at us both.

"But…" Jules chirps.

The door is now closed. Davis says a little louder, never taking his eyes from mine, "Bye, Jules."

Chapter 19: NOW-Still in Hiding

We haven't really left the room since Friday night. Davis ran out to get the coffee yesterday. The pizza guy brought dinner last night. In between, we have been living off whatever is in my room for food. At one point, Davis went to the vending machine to get me a Diet Coke. I think he may have side-tripped to Charlie's room, because he hasn't run out of condoms and I hate to think he arrived with as many as we've used. The thought makes me giggle, but also brings up a few things I need to discuss with him.

It's the early hours of Sunday morning and still dark outside. The sun isn't threatening to come out yet. The lights from the parking lot are the only thing illuminating the room. Davis' iPod is playing softly. We are lying there. In the semi-dark. Semi-dressed. Wrapping around each other, stroking each other's skin. When Davis hears me giggle, he asks in a deep, sleepy, sexy voice, "What's so funny?"

"The condoms," I tell him.

"Since when are condoms funny?"

"You haven't run out and we've been in here a long time."

He tells me exactly what I suspected, "I may have dropped by Charlie's room when I went out." I giggle a bit more.

"That's what I was giggling about. You asking Charlie. Did he warn you again?" I ask.

"Of course. He's very protective of you. I'm glad he is."

"Mavis, even though I was laughing….I was also wondering…"

"Yeah?"

"Well, you know about me…about my…"

"Sexual history?" Davis finishes my thought.

"Yeah."

He sighs. "And you want to know about mine?"

"If you don't mind telling me."

"Lizard, I don't mind telling you anything. I just don't want it to change how you feel about me once you hear it. It's not something I am proud of. Maybe I was at one time. But not now. Now that I have you." It is such a declaration.

I need to reassure him. "You know pretty much everything I've done. I just think we should both know. To be safe." I cringe internally. I have told him everything...everything I remember.

I don't really enjoy hearing it, but I know I need to. Davis was promiscuous beginning at age 16. He never lacked for girlfriends or sex, which doesn't surprise me. He's incredibly attractive, mysterious, quiet at times, but then, at times he can be outrageously flirty. I'd seen him that way with me. Briefly with others. I knew he'd pulled back from flirting with anyone else recently. I could easily imagine him charming the pants off anyone he chose to. He became engaged to Kathleen after his brother died, when he finally went to college, but the engagement didn't stop his fooling around. He struggled with why, but he felt he was looking for something. He tried to find it with Kathleen, but it wasn't enough. When he moved to Weldon, nothing much changed. He had his pick of available and ready girls. There seemed no need to change.

"Then I went to Charlie's room one day before fall semester. I saw that picture of you with him. He explained it. Told me and Jake, unfortunately, about you. Some of the crazy plans you and he had when you were bartending. How you and Charlie kissed and it just didn't feel right. How you shut him down." I laughed out loud at the memory of that ill-fated hook-up attempt with Charlie. We liked each other, just, no chemistry, like kissing your brother. Davis continued, "You looked so happy and mischevious in that picture. Cute and sexy and fun. Someone to talk to and be goofy with. Charlie's stories about you confirmed it. Who thinks to do something like re-inact the movie, Less than Zero? And the fact that you turned down Charlie, I mean, come on, Charlie's pretty hot. I'm a dude and even I think so. Then I met you the next day in the cafeteria. I thought you were so adorable. I couldn't stop looking at you. I was dying for you to look in my eyes. When you did, your eyes just slayed me. I saw flashes of the Biz that Charlie described, but I also saw the hurt. I didn't know everything then, just the little bit Charlie had told us about Neil breaking up with you so publicly. Still, I wanted to take away the hurt. I wanted to see you smile, make you laugh. I told myself you were off-limits, but I couldn't stay away. Then you got the job at The

Space. It was like you were being sent to me. I was with a lot of girls before, I admit that. I was always looking for you, I think. I think I loved you before I met you. Wow, that sounds crazy!"

He knew he loved me? He knew back then?

"You weren't... but you were...what about Kathleen? Opening night?" I am truly confused. He had to have been with her then.

"Ahh, Opening night... You mean Hell on Earth night." Davis intones sarcastically.

Hell on Earth for me, yes. "What do you mean, Hell on Earth?" I quiz.

"Are you kidding? Seeing you with Jake like that. Him all over you. You seeming to want him. I was a mess. When I made eye contact with you on the street from my car, I snapped. I told Kathleen I had forgotten something in the lobby of Lawrence Hall. I waited until I saw you and Jake walk in the side door. Then I went in with a bunch of people and, pretending to be drunk, fell against the fire pull station and yanked it. I turned around and left. I don't think anyone saw me. I know you are an RA and might need to report me, but I don't care. You need to know. I had to do something. Something to slow you down with Jake. Something to make you stop and think. Something. Anything. I don't even know if it worked." I've never heard Davis say so much at once.

Becoming very quiet and serious, I tell Davis it did work. That I didn't have sex with Jake. His face is overcome with a look of relief and joy. He pulls me in for a kiss. Knowing I wasn't with Jake has made him very happy.

"Davis, I haven't been with anyone since last May. And I won't report you for the fire alarm," I tease. "I'm glad you did it. It is the most romantic thing anyone has done for me. Exceptionally weird and risky, but romantic."

Continuing his kisses down my shoulder he tells me, "I'm so glad it worked."

"Lizard, I didn't sleep with Kathleen that night either."

"You didn't?"

Davis reassures me, "No, we had a huge fight. She was beginning to suspect something wasn't right. Not about you in particular, but she knew I'd been unfaithful before. She sensed that I didn't love her. She got so angry she packed her stuff and made me take her to the train station. She said she needed time to think. When we talked again over winter break, we both knew it was over."

I have to ask. Not knowing is killing me. I collect myself for what I am about to ask and what I am almost sure the response will be.

"Thanksgiving, Davis. Did you sleep with her over Thanksgiving?" He is still holding me, but all movement, all the soft strokes and kisses we have been sharing throughout this conversation cease. Davis turns his head away to look toward the wall.

"Yes." His voice is shaky.

Small tears slide down my face before I am even aware. "I think I already knew that."

Turning back to me slowly, I see he is tearful, too. He reaches up tentatively, as if I would stop him, and wipes my tears away with his thumb. "I did. She was my fiancée. I wasn't sure if I could ever have you. I thought you were with Jake and I owed it to Kathleen to try. I …I was incredibly weak. It may not make you feel better, but I did nothing but think of you the whole time I was with her."

I understand. I did the same thing the times I made out with Jake.

I sniffle. Tears drop onto Davis' chest. I rub them away with my fingers and then lean over to kiss where they landed. He pulls me into his chest. Tilting my head up to look at his beautiful, sad face, I tell him, "I will never like it, but I understand." I can't control the soft sobs I'm breathing onto his chest.

"Biz, I already knew I wanted you, loved you. I should have been stronger. I am so, so sorry."

"You don't have to apologize anymore, Davis. I really do understand. More than you know. I want to make sure we are safe, you know?"

"We are. I've always used a condom, because of my lifestyle. Even with Kathleen. How about you?"

I swallow a few times. Time to be honest. "Like I said, I haven't been with anyone since May. I was tested over the summer and everything was negative. But, Davis, you have to know, I wasn't always so "with it" when I was with some of those random guys. Oh my god, I can't even remember the las…" Before I can finish the thought, Davis hushes me.

"It's going to be fine. We are together now. We'll use protection. We'll get tested, together. It's going to be all right."

I can't believe he is being so cool about all this. I know he must be upset and angry on some level. I am. With myself.

"All that really matters is that we are together. We'll just figure it out, okay? Can you do this with me. Can you let go and trust me to take care of you? Us?

I nod my head against his hard chest and stroke my hand across his rippled abs and sigh. *Trust him.* Allowing myself to relax into him after this extremely difficult and enlightening discussion, I drift and am asleep before I know it.

Chapter 20: NOW-Coming Out

Coffee. I smell coffee and hear water running. Davis has already gotten up and gone down to get me coffee and must be in the shower. I've always harbored a secret theory that heaven would be like drinking coffee while taking a shower and having sex. Now is as good a time as any to test that theory. I reach over to my nightstand and grab the coffee. Still on my tummy, I tilt my head back and take a long slow sip. Perfect, as usual. I need to remind myself to ask Davis how he always gets it right. I've never told him how I like my coffee.

I don't have anything on, so I take my coffee and my nakedness and hop out of the loft bed. Reaching my bathroom door, I slowly open it to hear Davis singing a power love ballad by a group that is more known for fast heavy tunes. I haven't heard him sing except for his drunken sing-along with Jake the night of the kegger. The bathroom is steamy and smells like my apple body wash. Before putting my cup down, I take one more sip of coffee and then slip into the shower behind him. He doesn't jump or startle, just stops singing, hums, and pushes back slightly into me as come up behind him to wrap my arms around his waist and rest my cheek on his muscular back.

"You're singing. You sound happy," I tell him.

"I am. I used to always sing when I was happy. Drove my brother crazy."

I ask, "Were you happy when you were singing to me drunkenly the night of the keg party?"

"Yes….and just between you and me….I wasn't drunk."

"Yes you were, I was there. You were hammered."

"Nope, I might have been a little buzzed, but not drunk. Jake was drunk. That was my plan." He is confessing to tricking me. I feign disgust, but really I am flattered.

I run my hands up and down his rock-hard abs and tease a bit lower with my pinkies.

"You acted drunk, to get Jake drunk, to get rid of him, so I would take care of you?"

"And it worked, I got to sleep with you."

I reach lower and stroke his now fully formed erection. He tilts his head back and rests it on my shoulder, as I touch him. I hear him moan his approval of the move.

"You didn't sleep with me."

"Sure I did. I slept in your room, with you. Jake didn't. That was good enough for me. I just wanted to be close. Can you forgive my deception?"

I think he knows I'll forgive him. I have him in a pretty vulnerable position. My hand is wrapped around his throbbing cock and I am stroking upward firmly.

"I think I might need some sort of demonstration of remorse for your deception," I groan into his ear. Along with his hardness in my hand, the steam and warm water are causing me to slick up as I grind against his ass. Davis spins around in my arms and pushes me up against the back wall of the shower. The water is pounding over his shoulders, causing a waterfall between us. He reaches down to stroke my clit, causing me to cry out.

"I am so very remorseful, please forgive me." Davis begs as he slips two fingers into me and circles inside finding my G-spot. His thumb has moved back to my clit.

It's my turn to beg. As I begin to release onto his hand, I cry out, "You are forgiven…now please, I want you inside me." He inhales sharply through his teeth, causing a hissing noise, removes his fingers, grabs my ass, lifts me up against the wall and pushes his hardness into me.

"I. Love. That. You. Forgive. Me." He says one word with each thrust. Rocking into each other, we build to a gloriously loud pinnacle. Once we are both calmer, he pulls out and slides me down so I'm standing in front of him again. I hold onto his arms to steady myself, because our exertion has left me a bit lightheaded.

Leaning down to lick some drops of water off my ear and kiss below it, he husks hotly, "That little deception was totally worth it. Then and now."

What can I do? He is adorable. Sneaky, but adorable. And so handsome, naked and wet in my shower.

We dry each other off. I begin dressing. Davis is putting on the clothes he had on when he came to my rescue on Friday. We both look at them and then each other.

"I think I need to go to my place and change clothes."

"I would loan you my Hello Kitty PJ pants, but they would probably be too small and people would stare." I tease him.

"Ya think?"

"Probably."

Davis offers a compromise, "How about you finish getting dressed, I'll run home and change and meet you downstairs for brunch at noon?"

I openly pout, but agree to the plan. "I hate for you to leave, but you can't exactly live in the same clothes all weekend."

He kisses me soundly. As he moves to open the door he assures me, "I'll be back before you miss me."

Once the door closes behind him, I whisper to myself, "You're wrong, I miss you already." Then I smile and do a happy dance around my tiny dorm room.

***

Already clean from the best-shower-I-ever-had-in-my-life, I quickly dress in jeans and a cute hot pink long-sleeved thermal shirt, accessorized with a patterned infinity scarf. It's getting cold outside and if we actually ever go out somewhere I will need to be warm. I dry my hair quickly and throw on a bit of light make-up. I want my day with Davis to be relaxed. I don't want to be uncomfortable or fussy at all. I have a bit over an hour before I need to meet Davis downstairs. Switching on my laptop, I decide to do something I don't normally do. I Google. I haven't thought to do it before, and in hindsight probably should have plenty of other times... with Neil, Jake. It just never crossed my mind. Something Davis said before Thanksgiving has come back to the forefront of my brain. Curiosity is getting the better of me. Davis told me his brother died and his dad was in some sort of accident. I type Davis' name into the search bar. There are some articles from his high school about the technical theatre stuff he's done. Under images, I see his face. Plenty of red party cup pictures of him...and girls. More than a few with girls. Younger, but him. A little further down, there appears to be part of a funeral notice from about six years ago, for Cole Brandon. Reading through it I hit on the following words and phrases, DIED

215

SUDDENLY...SURVIVED BY HIS PARENTS, LT. GOVERNOR

JAMES AND MEREDITH AND AN OLDER BROTHER, DAVIS.

Oh my god, Davis wasn't kidding when he was talking about pain.

Died Suddenly? That's code, funeral notice code for murder or suicide

or a car accident. Accident? Davis said his dad was in an accident.

I type JAMES BRANDON LT. GOVERNOR in the search

bar. There are tons of hits. Under NEWS is an article describing how

Former Lt. Governor James Brandon of Illinois has recovered from his

spinal cord injury from a gunshot wound, but will be partially

paralyzed. GUN SHOT WOUND? He is now serving as a consultant

on various issues including gun control and mental health issues, for

the current governor of Illinois. I scan a bit further down the page. I

open up the page of images for James Brandon. There are pictures of

a very handsome man that looks like an older version of Davis. In

some, he is by himself. In others, he is greeting people in a receiving

line, with what appears to be his wife, Davis and Kathleen. They are

obviously well dressed. Wealthy. These are society page photos.

And then another picture grabs and holds my attention. It's Mr. and

Mrs. Brandon, Davis, Kathleen, and Cole, but in this picture, Cole has

his arm around Kathleen and she is snuggled into him. I click on the picture and read the caption. "Lt. Governor and Mrs. Brandon, his older son, Davis, and younger son, Cole, along with Cole's girlfriend, Miss Kathleen Holbrook.

I am dizzied by the amount of information I have found in such as short amount of time. Davis' ex-fiancee was Cole's girlfriend? Mr. Brandon was injured by a gunshot wound? Cole Brandon died suddenly? Davis must have been through hell a few years ago. This is the "long story" he inferred before Thanksgiving. It's overwhelming. I need to find Davis. He deserves my support and understanding. I feel like an idiot. My issues are NOTHING compared to what he's been through.

I throw on my tall black Uggs. I can't find my winter coat, so I put on my fleece jacket. Davis should be down in the cafeteria soon. I will go down there and wait for him. Perhaps we can eat quickly and leave or sneak off to a corner of the cafeteria and talk. It will be up to him. I will just be there for him. I am beginning to get a clearer picture of why Davis is the way he is. He is quiet, a bit moody, and can be stoically intimidating to some people. I have seen flashes of anger. I suspect he punched out Jake. But he is also incredibly protective of those he cares about. He put off college to care for his parents. I wonder exactly what happened six years ago?

Pulling the door shut on my dorm room, I spin around to come face to face with a sour looking Suzette.

"I came by to thank you, Biz." she simpers in a fake way.

I have no time for this. I need to find Davis. "Thank me, for what?"

"Breaking up with Jake. I mean, he was about to do it anyway, but, well, even though he's hot in the sack, he deserved you knocking him on his ass. Now he won't be so worried about sneaking around. It'll make hooking up so much easier."

God, she sounds so gross. Who actually thinks like that? I thought I had no respect for myself.

"That's fine, Suzette, whatever, good luck….I need to go find Davis," I flippantly bark out and go to move on.

"So you're with Davis, huh? I was wondering who you were screwing in there. You weren't exactly quiet. You don't know much about Davis, do you? I do. I'm from near his hometown. His parents are going to HATE you. And he is going to HATE that you are

CRAZY. Especially after his brother went nuts and tried to kill him. He'll dump your ass in no time."

What? What was that about Cole trying to kill Davis. Oh my god. I need to find Davis now.

I am starting to get pissed and trying hard not to cry. "I'm not crazy."

"Oh, really…Not what I heard from Randall."

Shit, she knows Randall? She knows why I left town.

"You know Randall?"

"Sure, through Neil. I've known Neil for years. We were RAs together before you came along. Banged him before you did. He and Randall are really 'good friends'-almost like brothers," she snarks with a laugh. "Have a little 'business' going on." I must have a confused look on my face, because she continues, "Oh, looks like you didn't know about that." Suzette cackles, "You will soon enough, you naïve bitch."

"What?" I am completely lost. All I can think about is Davis almost getting killed.

Suzette keeps talking, "I'm just saying, once Davis finds out everything about your summer…about you losing your mind and

219

running away, By the way, Randall still wants that $500… your little love affair will be history."

"Davis already knows." I lie. I lie right to her face. Davis doesn't know about my crack up, not all of it. He doesn't know about my concerns about that last night at Randall's. The thing I can't remember.

Suzette smirks and twitches her eyebrows up. "Oh, sure he does… or maybe he doesn't and I should tell him…Anyway, just came by to thank you for cutting Jake loose. Have a great day." Suzette almost skips off, with a grin on her face like the fucking sugar plum fairy that delivered a bag of shit.

Find Davis. No, run. I don't really know which of these actions I am taking, I only know I am on the move. Down the main staircase of Lawrence Hall and out the front door. Oh my god, it's colder than I thought it was! Fine. It will help me think. Do I run away and figure this out on my own? Do I find Davis? I don't know. I'm so panicked, I can't even cry. I just know my heart is racing a ba-zillion miles an hour. What did Dr. Matt tell me? Oh, yeah, it will all be over in five minutes. Five minutes. That feels like a long time.

Stop, Biz!

Okay, I'm stopped. Now, what to do? I must not be paying any attention to anything else, just pacing and then stopping and squatting and holding my chest over and over, because I don't acknowledge anything or anyone in my environment, until I see a large black SUV squeal up beside me. Davis. It's Davis' Escalade.

I look up and lock onto his eyes when I hear the window buzz down.

"Lizard, what are you doing?" he asks. He looks scared. Why is he scared?

Because you are pacing and breathing rapidly, idiot. You probably look like you've seen a ghost. You look....crazy.

"Umm... I just came out to…" I can't articulate what I don't know.

"Run?"

"No, I was going to look for you and then I was ambushed."

"Ambushed? Wait. Stay right where you are. I'm parking the car. Don't move."

I do what he says. Something about someone else taking over; telling me what to do helps to calm me. Oh no, he really must think I looked crazy pacing around out here like an animal. How am I going

221

to explain this morning and my confrontation with Suzette to him? My initial concern is for him. His feelings. What he has gone through. It must have been traumatic from the little I am piecing together. Suzette's comments, though, they just unhinged me. She's probably right. He's so much better than me. Kathleen is better than me. How can we possibly work?

I remain right where Davis told me to stay. I'm pretty sure my eyes are huge and terrified, if his expression is reflecting any of what I feel. I am way in my head. Putting both of his hands on my upper arms, Davis half squats down to make eye contact and pull me back to reality. "What the hell happened?"

I don't know why I say it, but all I can think to reply is, "I Googled you."

Davis barks out a soft laugh, "Well, if that's what you want to call what we've been doing the past couple of days... Googling."

His joking shocks me and I unexpectedly laugh, too, in the middle of my panic. "I didn't mean it as a euphemism," I joke back. "I really Googled you, and your dad."

Realization of what I have possibly uncovered spreads across his face and the levity of the Google joke completely vanishes. "Oh," is all he says. "What do you know?"

"I read a bunch. It was a little confusing, but I think I've pieced it together. I was going to the cafeteria to find you. I wanted to be there for you. To have you explain it all to me, so I would understand you better... And then, Suzette appeared and ambushed me outside my door."

Davis now looks more panicked than I just did. "What did she say?"

"She thanked me for dumping Jake." Davis snorts in response to that bit of information. "She then proceeded to tell me how I'd never be good enough for you, that I'm crazy and that, that in itself, would drive you away. She knows a lot about Neil....and Randall. I... I got scared. I just had to move. I didn't even know if I was running to find you or to run away from you. You know, remove myself before you found out how damaged I really am. I...I...."

Davis wraps me in his arms very tightly. "You're shaking. You're cold. I think you are having a panic attack. Let's get you inside. Do you need anything?"

Part of me wants to say, "my Xanax," but I haven't needed them since this summer. Instead I tell him, "I don't know what I need. That's the problem."

Davis moves, grabbing my hand tightly, almost too tightly, and pulls me inside the lobby of Lawrence. We fly through the halls and make our way to the cafeteria. It's pretty busy with the brunch crowd. *Oh no, not the cafeteria. Not a scene in the cafeteria.* Right as we move through the cafeteria doors, I pull back on his hand. It takes all of my strength, because Davis is really upset and it's manifesting itself physically. His muscles are tense all over and he practically growls as I pull back hard.

"What, Biz?"

"Davis, please, I don't want a scene. I know you are mad, but I can't take any more attention. Please. Slow down and breathe."

Still growling slightly, but taking deep breaths, Davis finally speaks, "I am only calming down because you are asking me to, Lizard. Right now, I want to tear down these walls and go after anyone that scared you. Made you panic."

"I'm better now. Now that you're here. But could you loosen up on my hand a bit? I think I'm losing circulation." I try to make a joke to make him smile.

"Oh, god, baby, I am so sorry." He loosens his grip, runs his thumb gently over the top of my hand and then brings it to his mouth to kiss my knuckles. Looking intently into my eyes, he tells me, "I am going to say something to Suzette and Jake and anyone else here that thinks they need to know. I am going to tell them exactly what is going on with you…and me. Can you stick with me?" I nod yes.

Much calmer now, Davis and I move to our group's table. Everyone is there. Even the off-campus people. Davis acknowledges everyone. I just keep my gaze on him most of the time, but cast a brief glance toward Charlie and Jules.

Davis stares right at Suzette. He is whispering, not yelling, but his voice is low and threatening. He is not up in her face. He is just staring down at her like she is some sort of insignificant bug. "Suzette, I will not tolerate you harassing my girlfriend." Suzette inhales and everyone's attention at the table moves to watch the exchange between Davis and Suzette. "Biz has never done anything to you. She's with me now. I. LOVE. HER. Nothing you do or say or think you know

225

about her matters. She has me. I will do anything to protect her. Anything. Get it?" He shifts his attention to Jake. "Jake, I'd be careful, man. Suzette might be more than you can handle." He jerks his thumb back to indicate Suzette, "Good luck with THAT." He doesn't say "good luck" or "that" in a positive way. Davis basically told Jake he's screwed.

Neither Suzette nor Jake say a word. The rest of our table starts clapping and cheering. Jules jumps up and hugs both Davis and me. Charlie comes to give me a kiss on the cheek. Davis playfully shoves him away and pulls me tighter. Charlie congratulates Davis by slapping him on the back. When I pull myself away from my best friend's hug and look back, Jake and Suzette have vanished from our table. Good riddance.

After eating brunch with our friends, Davis turns to me and whispers in my ear that it's time to go. I've almost…almost let all the information I found out this morning wash away in the happiness of him announcing "Us" to our friends and setting Jake and Suzette straight. We say our goodbyes.

Davis tells the entire table, "Yeah, we gotta go…Google." Oh My God! Everyone at the table just nods and grins like he means the real Google, but I know when he says Google he means what we've been hiding in my dorm room doing, "Google." I roll my eyes at the ceiling and embarrassed, say, "Davis!"

"What? They don't know when I say Google, I mean sex." he informs me loudly and pointedly.

Charlie chimes in. "Well, now we do." Davis and I leave amidst our friends laughter and my blushing. Davis is loving it.

Chapter 21: NOW-The Storm

Davis ushers me out of the cafeteria, out of the building and to the parking lot with his hand on the small of my back. I love being touched by him there. We move toward his car. I thought we'd just go back to my room, but evidently we are headed somewhere else.

"Where are we going?" I ask.

"To my place. I think we need to talk."

"Uh oh, good talk or bad talk?" I wonder aloud.

Not giving up much information he says, "We'll see."

Davis has told me he loves me, he's told all his friends he loves me, but right now he sounds cryptic. A bit somber. This makes me extremely anxious. I start blabbing as we drive to his house.

"I can't believe you talked to Suzette like that. Just told her you loved me. Just like that. No one, ever, except my dad, has ever protected me like that. And you... you called me your girlfriend. I've never had anyone call me their girlfriend. Well, not that I ever heard." Once again, I cannot shut up. I chatter the entire short drive to his place. Throughout the drive, Davis is looking straight out the windshield and occasionally shaking his head. I wonder what he is thinking, but not enough to shut up. I'm too nervous and excited. If I shut up there will only be awkward silence.

We pull up to an older looking building in the Central West End area of town. It's really nice. Nicer than most college students can afford. That's right, Davis is wealthy. That's something else we will have to talk about. The thoughts in my head come right out of my mouth, "Wow, Davis. This place is gorgeous. What is it, apartments, condos?"

Davis shuts off the car, looks over at me with his stunning green eyes, but he says nothing. He turns away from me, gets out of the car and walks around to my side. He opens my door and stands

looking down at me.

"Davis, what's wrong? Why won't you talk to me? I thought

you said we needed to talk?"

He reaches in, grabs my hand, and pulls me up out of the car

and into his arms. Davis warmly breathes into my ear.

"Lizard…Baby… you and that chatter…you are KILLING. ME."

This makes me laugh with relief and amusement. He continues, "You

have got to stop talking or you are going to have me so hard, we'll

never talk. I won't be able to tell you all I need to tell you." He finally

smiles. Oh, he's not mad or upset. Thank god. I'm just turning him

on. The thought tickles me. I can turn him on by talking in my

strange excited way. He must really like me…Love me.

"No more talking," Davis murmurs slowly in my ear with

mock seriousness, "from you anyway."

"I'm shutting up now." I then make a motion with my hand in

front of my mouth, like I'm locking my lips with a key

"Uh huh." With that Davis scoops me up in his arms and

carries me into the vestibule of his building. He sets me down and

never taking his eyes off of mine, reaches down to take my hand. He then tugs me gently to follow him up to the second floor. Moving to a door toward the front of the building he turns and tells me, "This is me," and points to the door with the number 2B.

Entering his place, I am shocked. This is definitely not a college student's home. There is a small entry way spilling into a large open space. At the front of the room are two large floor- to-ceiling bay windows separated by a large wall with a flat screen television over a fireplace. Out of the window you can see Forest Park. There are two comfy-looking couches in chocolate brown and a large chair with an ottoman facing the fireplace. Across the large space are a set of french doors that are slightly open. An elaborate open kitchen is behind a large granite-topped island with barstools in front. Between one of the sofas and the island, a bit off to the side, is a dining room table with seating for eight. I wonder how much more there is to this place.

"You're rich." It comes out as sort of a question and a statement.

Davis looks around the room and then at me, "My parents are well off."

"I always wondered about the new car and expensive watch and stuff. Other than that, you don't come off as wealthy."

"Like I said, I'm not wealthy, my parents are… All of this," he gestures around his condo, apartment, whatever it is, "is…I don't know, something between taking care of me, a bribe and guilt."

"I don't get it." I say, puzzled.

"You will." Davis takes my hand and walks me to the large chair with the ottoman. He sits me down in it and then sits on the ottoman in front of me. There is tension in his beautiful face. His eyes seem dull, the usual spark extinguished in them. "I'm going to tell you everything, but I don't think I can sit by you or touch you while I do. It will be too easy to distract myself and you. I'll never get through it."

I admit, I'm a little hurt that he can't be near me. It worries me a little. Davis moves across to one of sofas, away from me.

"My brother Cole and I were best friends. Really close. I am only 15 months older than him. We did everything together. Toward the middle of his junior year of high school, Cole changed. He was usually happy, a good student, a good boyfriend to Kathleen. That's right, Kathleen was Cole's girl." Davis clarifies the last part when I

232

make a face. "Suddenly, Cole started sleeping all day, missing school, telling our parents he didn't feel good. He'd stay up all night, out with friends we didn't know well. He started ignoring Kathleen. Defying our parents. You can imagine this did not go over well with the current Lt. Governor and possible future candidate for governor of Illinois. I admit, at first, I didn't pay much attention to the differences. Even though we were close, I was a tied up with my senior year. I was focused on getting into college, and of course, my social life. I didn't have or want a girlfriend, but there was no shortage of girls to hook up with." Davis shakes his head and looks in my eyes apologetically. "One night, I heard Cole come home late, actually early in the morning. I heard him finally go to his room. It got quiet, so I thought he had gone to sleep, but then I heard him crying. Not gentle crying. Loud, heaving sobs. That wasn't usual at all for Cole. I went to his room. He didn't say anything when I went in and sat on his bed. He was fully clothed, lying in a ball, hugging a pillow. I asked him what was wrong. Do you know what he said?" I shake my head no. "He said he didn't know. I didn't understand how someone could be that miserable and not know why. I asked him questions about school, Kathleen, his schedule. Again, he said he really didn't know, only that

233

suddenly everything seemed difficult. It was difficult to get out of bed. Difficult to talk to Kathleen. He said he was working hard to feel happy, but he wasn't happy out with his new friends. It was just a distraction, something different, but even that wasn't working anymore. I didn't know anything about mental health at the time. I wish I had, because I might have been able to help him. My parents and I found out later, too late, that Cole was bipolar."

"Too late?" I ask. "You mean, the accident?" I say "the accident" because I have an idea of what is coming next, but I don't want to guess. I want Davis to tell me. His expression is not one of surprise when I say "accident."

Davis continues, telling me the whole story. Cole continued to go downhill. His parents tried to get him to a psychiatrist, but he refused, saying it would get better. He wouldn't allow his parents to put him on medication. That junior year was just hard. He missed a lot of school. Kathleen started coming over about an hour or two before Cole's late afternoon/evening wake-up time. He was cold to her. She would try to talk to him, to get him to go somewhere with her. He would tell her he had other plans. Plans that they later found out included going out and "self-medicating" with his newfound friends. Davis and Kathleen started spending the time before Cole

would emerge together, worrying about Cole, plotting ways to help

him. Kathleen was over at their house waiting on a night in early May.

Davis' parents were out of town at a benefit and would return in the

morning. Cole did his usual. He woke up, paid only the most cursory

attention to Kathleen and then took off. Kathleen was upset and

crying telling Davis that she didn't know what else to do and she

thought maybe she should break up with Cole. Davis held her and

comforted her. Nothing more. They fell asleep together on the sofa in

Davis' parent's family room. Cole returned at around 9:00 in the

morning and found them asleep together. He went ballistic. Started

accusing Kathleen of "hooking up" with Davis. Saying that was the

only reason why she was always over at the house. He verbally

attacked Davis, using every instance of Davis' promiscuity against him

as evidence that he was sleeping with Kathleen. Davis and Kathleen

both tried to calm him, telling him none of what he thought was true.

Cole could not be reasoned with. He ran and locked himself in the

garage. Davis knew the family guns were in there. He didn't think

Cole would go that far, but he couldn't take any chances. Chasing

Cole to the door, just as he locked it, Davis turned to Kathleen and

235

ordered her to look on the key hook for keys that might fit the garage lock. Davis tried talking to Cole through the door, but Cole wasn't answering. All Davis could hear were things being frantically moved around.

"After that, everything happened very quickly," Davis elaborates. "When I recall it, it's in horrifyingly slow motion, but at the time it was mere moments." Davis' voice is full and heavy. I have tears welling up, but I am looking up trying to keep them from falling. I return my gaze to Davis. The pain in his face is transparent. This is so devastating for him to recall. I stand to go to him.

"No, stay there. I need to finish. Let me finish first." Davis exhales. There is a small moan of sadness along with it. I sit back down.

"Kathleen never found the key. I became desperate, so I kicked at the door. I just kept kicking until I made a hole large enough to reach through and unlock the garage door. I opened the door to see two things: The outside garage door opening as my parent's car drove in and Cole, standing at the back of the garage. He had one of my father's handguns and was loading it. Cole leveled the gun at me, screaming that I had stolen Kathleen away from him; that nothing was

236

worth living for. He said a lot of things that weren't true and didn't make sense. That our parents were trying to send him away, that an angel told him. None of his delusions were true. I was scared, but I stepped toward him..." Davis is crying, but determined to continue. I want to stop Davis, stop the painful story and hold him. I know he won't let me, so I stay in my chair, captive to the story. "Cole fired the gun...he fired it... at me, but it didn't hit me. My father in those few moments had gotten out of the car, run to the back of the garage and moved toward Cole to disarm him. He was too late, so he stepped in front of the gun, just as Cole fired it at me. He caught it by the barrel with one hand and moved the gun down. The bullet hit him in the spine. He fell to the floor. I ran to my father. There was so much blood and he was so pale. I knelt over and held him. All Dad said was, 'The gun, get the gun.' I was just beginning to comprehend that he meant get the gun from Cole. I looked up and the gun was still pointed down at my father and me." Davis can no longer contain his anguish. He is standing up pacing and crying. My poor Davis. "Cole was weeping, talking and crying harder than I've ever seen anyone in my life....he...he put the gun in his mouth and, Biz, he...Oh, My

God…he…shot himself. In front of all of us. Mom. Kathleen. Dad. Me. Cole killed himself."

I don't care what Davis told me anymore, I can't stand to see him standing on the other side of the room, so alone. I rush over to him. He stops his pacing and holds me with eyes. It's a look I've never seen from Davis. He is shattered. He carries this around with him all the time.

"Oh, my god, Davis. You've been through so much. Oh my god." We are both heaving and crying, holding tightly to each other. I don't know how, but I somehow move us to a sofa. We sit there. Me trying to assimilate all the information. Davis trying to stop crying. As we slowly calm, I gather the courage to ask, "What happened next?" Maybe it will be easier for him to tell me more if I am holding him. I know it will be easier for me.

Davis slowly, in stops and starts between sobs and heavy exhalations, finishes the story. "It's all a fog. Mom or Kathleen called 911, I don't know who. I stayed in the garage, holding my dad and talking to him to so he'd stay conscious. I just sat there holding him and occasionally looking over at my brother's dead body. There was so much blood. Some gray stuff. I tried not to look, but I kept glancing over. Eventually, the police, an ambulance and the coroner arrived. I was moved to the house by the police. I must have been in shock, because my memory of the next few hours is very spotty. My mother, Kathleen and I answered a million questions, as my father was stabilized and taken to the nearest trauma center. Cole's body was removed by the coroner. The police eventually left. The media was not far behind. It was a nightmare for all of us. Biz, we didn't know. We didn't know how sick Cole was. We just had no idea he could have a psychotic break." I am feeling incredibly guilty. I have to let Davis know that I have mental health issues. I am sure he won't want to deal with that again. I can't let this, us, go on, if it will hurt him in anyway. I just have to find the right time.

It wasn't his fault. He has to know that. "Davis, Cole's illness, it wasn't your fault." I gently whisper to him between soft sobs.

"That's what everyone says. My father tells me he feels lucky he didn't lose both of us. How can he feel that way when he is in a wheelchair for life?"

"It's amazing what we'll do...for someone we love." My head is on his shoulder and I look up to see a small sad smile on Davis' lips, followed by a cleansing sigh. He hugs me tighter.

"Do you understand more, now? Is it a little clearer?" he asks.

"Yes." It's clear to me. Davis and I might not work out. If we do, it will take work, a bunch of work.

***

It starts snowing around 4:30 in the afternoon. I can see it out the bay windows. We have been sitting on the sofa for two hours or more. Not talking, just holding each other. I need to tell Davis about my breakdown. I need to tell him that I am not stable. It can't wait. I need to do it now.

I pull away from Davis. He isn't making it easy, keeping a firm grip on me and saying, "Uh.. where are you going?"

"I have to be able to look at you. Look you in the eyes. There are things you need to know about me...." I am about to reveal details about my summer and treatment, when Davis' cell phone rings.

He looks at the number. "It's my mother. I said good-bye, but left the house a little abruptly to come back to school. I think I need to talk to her." Tilting his head, he frowns and squints his eyes in apology. I indicate that he should take it.

"Hey, Mom...Yes, I know I left quickly." He looks at me. "I needed to get back and take care of something. Yes...it's true….Kathleen and I broke up….I'm sorry you don't understand…" I can't listen to anymore. He was with Kathleen for a long time. After his brother died she was there for him. She is almost already part of the Brandon family. Those kind of attachments don't just go away.

I move off the sofa and away from Davis to look out the window. The snow is really coming down now. It's accumulating on the grass and the sidewalks. I didn't know this was coming, then again I haven't really been focused on the weather the past few days. Listening to Davis' phone conversation with his mother, I feel the panic starting. I need to get everything out in the open. I also need to get out. Davis is still on the phone, so I move toward the door. I left my Uggs and jacket on the table by the door. I walk over and put them on. I'm not running. I just need air.

Moving to open the door, I feel Davis behind me, still on the phone. Reaching over my shoulder, he puts his hand on the door in front of me, not allowing me to leave. He holds it shut. I turn my head to look at him questioningly and he frowns at me. He thinks I'm trying to run away. I shake my head no.

Davis stays on the phone with his mom, while trying to communicate with me non-verbally. "I know, I know Mom, I should have told you immediately. I realize you will have to manage the media. There is a perfectly good reason…Mom…Mom? I have to go. No, I have to go now. I'll call you later." He hangs up and pins me with a concerned stare. "Where do you think you are going? Are you running?"

"No, I don't think so…No…not running. Just need some space.. air."

"Hang on." Davis grabs his jacket. He takes my hand and walks me out of the building. The snow falling is beautiful. The air smells clean and refreshes me immediately. I can tell by his deep exhalation and relaxation of his hand in mine that Davis has noticed the atmospheric calm, too. We walk across the street to the park. The sidewalks aren't shoveled. It's been snowing for a short time, but there is already at least an inch on the ground. Looks like it could be a pretty heavy snowfall.

"So, why did you need to escape? Was the story too much? The phone call?" It's taken minutes for Davis to break the silence as we walk.

"That may have started it, but then I realized I needed to tell you something. I need to tell you more about the summer before we

242

go any farther. I need to give you a chance to choose to get out of this."

Davis stops walking suddenly, turns to me and takes my other hand, "What, What the hell are you saying to me? A chance to choose? What?"

"Davis, I am mentally ill."

"Lizard, no you're not."

"No, Davis. I am. I have panic disorder. I was diagnosed during the summer. I've worked really hard to get better, but I have to work at it every day. Especially when things are stressful or anxiety provoking."

"Like your interaction with Suzette. Or hearing all the information I just told you?"

"Yes, that or if I am feeling unsure, like I don't trust a person or a situation. This past summer that was everyone, except my parents." I am trying to get him to understand.

"Do you trust me?" he asks.

"Yes, I trust you, but I want you to be informed. You might not want to take me on. Your brother, your family. You've been through so much. I am still working on getting better, every day." I explain to Davis about my summer in therapy and group. Needing Xanax. I leave out my suspicions that Randall may have "done something" to me.

Davis interrupts me. "My family and Kathleen have nothing to do with us. Panic disorder is not bipolar. It's everywhere. I know more about mental illness now. You sought treatment. You are actively trying to get better. Don't you get it? I love you, Biz. Lizard, there is no choosing. I've already chosen you. That's it."

"Are you sure?" I barely finish the question as Davis brings both of my hands to his mouth and kisses them. Then he lets go of them and brings his hands to my face and pulls me to him for a kiss. A gentle, loving, reassuring kiss.

"Very sure. I'm no prize, Lizard. Now you know about Cole and my dad. I stayed home to 'help' with my father's recovery, but I was also a mess. Everyone deals with grief differently. I deferred college, but when I wasn't helping with my Dad, I was drinking and fucking around. When we had that talk yesterday, I wasn't kidding. I used girls. Hearing you talk about being used by guys is excruciating for me. To think I treated someone like that. I'll regret it forever. I hope that if you forgive me, on some level I will be forgiven for all the girls I may have hurt." Davis is so sincere, my heart is breaking.

"I feel a little stupid." I say. "I broke down over a bad relationship. Followed by idiotic choices. You have endured real pain, real loss and grief."

"Hey, don't do that. Don't minimize your pain. You made bad decisions. I made bad decisions. We were both trying to get rid of the hurt and hurt ourselves in the process. Neither one of us had more or less reason for that. Nobody has more of a right than another to feel a certain way."

Davis continues, "I AM sorry about Kathleen. She pulled me out of my funk. Got me to slow down on the drinking. She convinced me it was okay to leave my dad and go to college. I got engaged to her because it seemed like the right thing to do. Cole had asked me to take care of her. I felt like I owed them both, but I was never in love with her."

Recalling the phone call, I have to ask. "How do your mother and father feel about you breaking up with her?"

"Kathleen's parents have money. They are involved with my family politically. It will be a change. I suspect Kathleen never really

245

loved me either. We were just caught up in the emotion of Cole's death and turned to each other. Our parents will understand eventually."

We start walking again. The anxiety is overwhelming me, even with Davis' reassurances. I start babbling, "Davis, I completely understand if being with me is not the right thing for you. I mean, we just got together. We could stop this, I would hate it, I would be so sad, but I would do it. I would stop it, if you thought my panic disorder was too much work or you needed to be with...."

"LIZARD!!" His emphatic voice startles me out of my chatter. "No more. No more talk about not being together. I want you. I want us. I have never wanted anything more in my life. Being with you takes away all the pain. I feel like I get another chance at being happy when I'm with you."

"Why?" I ask. I can't imagine why. I'm not rich, I'm not a great beauty like Kathleen.

"Little Lizard baby, you don't even know how beautiful you are, do you?" I shake my head no. "You are beautiful to me, to every guy. I see them looking at you." I am thinking he is nuts. "No, I'm not nuts." How'd he know what I was thinking. Davis kisses me,

246

deeply this time. Biting my bottom lip and then parting them to give his tongue admission. I kiss him back hungrily. Pulling me closer to him, he lowers us down to the ground. We are in the snow. I open my eyes briefly to see snow in the limbs of the tree above us. It's like a dream. The snow is cold on my back, but Davis, kissing me, pressing his firm body down on me, is warming me in the most delicious way. After our day of confessions and traumatic tales, we give in to passion. Maybe as a coping mechanism, but that's not the only reason.

"You kiss me like you're falling in love" I tell Davis when we finally break from our kissing.

"Lizard, baby. I am."

I look into his beautiful, deep green eyes and let him know, "I love you, too."

Davis kisses me deeply again and even though it's cold and the snow is falling on us, in our hair and on our faces, I can feel Davis becoming aroused.

"We gotta go," he stills suddenly and tells me. He rolls over so he is lying beside me. I think he is panting a little. My body misses his warmth and everything else I was feeling.

"Where?"

"Back to my place. All this emotion. Kissing you. Your chatter… has me all riled up. And we gotta get get you out of those wet clothes." He looks over and smirks at me as he stands up.

"Oh, so you're concerned about my health?" I giggle.

"Whatever it takes to get you out of those clothes." His smile is irresistible. "And actually, I am more worried about my health, if I don't get next to your naked body soon."

As he pulls me to a stand, I push up into his arms and grind a bit against his hardness, "We wouldn't want that now, would we?" I give him a peck on the lips. Then I run. Run out of the park toward his condo. Davis catches up with me right before I get to the wide street in front of his condo and grabs my hand to stop me.

"Baby? Biz, slow down. Let's not get hit by a car or anything before we get home." I stop. Entwining my fingers in his, I put my head on his shoulder. When the light changes, we cross together.

***

Our jackets and boots are quickly off and piled in front of Davis' front door. I am shivering, but I'm not exactly sure it's from rolling around in the snow or excitement. For once, I am not talking up a storm.

"Well, you've seen most of the rest of the place. How about I show you the bedroom?"

Still not talking, I nod my agreement with the plan. Davis is behind me with his arms wrapped around me. He walks me toward the French doors on the other side of the room. So, that's what's behind those doors. As he pushes them open, I get an eyeful of what could only be called a sanctuary. There is yet another large bay window. A king size bed is positioned in the middle of it. The walls are a rich blue-gray. All the bedding is white. The furniture is dark brown. It's masculine, but romantic. Especially with the snow falling outside. I get enough time for a cursory survey of the inviting room before Davis, still behind me, begins kissing my neck, causing me to close my eyes and push my backside into his erection. I lift my arms up and reach around to the back of his head, tangling my fingers in his soft, silky hair. Davis' hands slide from my waist to the edge of my thermal shirt, pulling it up and over my head. His hands return to cup my breasts and his thumbs skate over my hardening nipples. The shivering I felt earlier is long gone. I feel myself flush. Davis spins me quickly so my nipples brush his chest. He still has his button up on. That won't do. I want to feel his chest against mine. I unbutton

249

his shirt so fast, I think I may have popped a button or two off. His mouth is on mine, kissing the corners, and then opening it to suck and stroke my tongue. I moan into him. His arms around me, he has undone my bra and has slid it between us to drop it on the floor. I can now feel the hard, rigid muscles of his upper body against mine. I want to be closer. I need to feel all of him. Davis backs me up until the backs of my legs are against the bed. I sit unexpectedly. Davis remains standing, but looks down at me. My lower abdomen heats as his stare melts any bit of concern or worry away. I want him now. I reach up to pull him down on the bed, but he has other ideas. Davis gets on his knees in front of me. Kissing me, he reaches over, unbuttons and unzips my jeans and in one move removes them along with my panties. I fall back on the bed naked, wanting him close. He stays at my legs, kissing up my thighs. Each side from my knee to my hip, before he kisses across to my clit. He stops and inhales deeply. Holding my legs apart, his tongue licks me tentatively. I am already so worked up I arch on the bed. He circles my clit with his tongue, sucks it powerfully, as I feel the build-up coming. His licking and teasing of my most sensitive area becomes more intense and he is grasping at my bottom, pulling it up toward him. I thread my hands into his hair. Yelling out his name, I let go. Release with a body-shattering shudder. He hums. I think he is pleased to have made me come. As I try to catch my breath, Davis reaches up and palms my breasts, while kissing up my body.

When he lifts his face from one of my breasts, I say, "Hi, Mavis."

Davis shakes his head, "Lizard, I am never gonna recover from you. I don't want to."

I have straddled his thigh and can feel the roughness of his jeans against my clit, causing me to want to grind again. His erection is rubbing against my hipbone.

"You have got to take those jeans off." I tell him.

"Why don't you help me." I push him up so he is kneeling above me. Sliding up to sit in front of him, I reach up and undo this jeans, appreciating the muscular V from his hips downward. As I slide his jeans off, I notice he is commando. I look up at him and raise an eyebrow.

"What? This afternoon didn't start out in a positive way, but it's ending better than I hoped."

"Mavis, you are so naughty."

"Tell me about it."

His erection is in front of me. Too good to pass up. I don't have much experience in this area, but for Davis, I am willing to give it a try. I wrap my fingers around the base and stroke upward. Sitting up into kneeling, I kiss the tip of his velvety hardness and then plunge my lips around it up to my fingers on the base. Licking and sucking, I feel Davis' hands in my hair, encouraging me. Suddenly, he stills and, moving his hand under my chin, pulls me up and off of him. Hey, I wasn't done yet.

"Yeah, Baby, I... We..." He's stuttering with arousal. He firmly slides me back onto my back, runs a hand down my body and then between my legs, pushing them apart. Once again, he's managed to procure a condom, evidently out of thin air. He rolls it onto himself. Kneeling over me, he rubs the head of his cock against my achy wetness. I am completely ready for him and he for me. With a slow, steady push he is in me. I clench around him causing him to groan, and then we move. Move like we've known each other forever. Like we loved each other before we met. It doesn't take long for me to get close again.

Between kisses, Davis orders me, "Hold on just a minute, baby. Just a…"

He doesn't finish the sentence as we both cry out, falling into our orgasms and grasping each other with all our souls.

***

Lying in Davis' bed, with our heads where our feet would usually be, Davis and I, completely naked and huddled next to each other, gaze out the window. Snow is continuing to fall and although I haven't looked out the window and down to the ground to check the accumulation, I know there must be a lot. There is hardly any noise from outside, apart from the occasional scraping of a snow plow. We've been in Davis's apartment since Sunday afternoon. It's Tuesday morning. We've gotten texts that school and work have been cancelled for the past two days. We are snowed in. It's the largest snowstorm this town has seen since the 80's. I'm under no delusion. We have a ton to talk about, a lot of work to do to be together, but right now with him in the quiet, I have never felt safer or happier.

WOO HOO! My "construction worker cat call" text alert goes off.

I reach over across Davis' chest, which puts me practically on top of him. I kiss his chest on way back to my spot with my phone in my hand and he runs his hand through my hair. Looking at the text, I shake my head and laugh. It's Jules, checking to make sure we are still alive AND to give her opinion about my future with Davis. Davis reaches for the phone. I move away from him to my side, to keep it away from him, but he somehow manages to flip me over, so I am now on my back and he is on top of me, head at my chest looking up at me.

"What's so funny?"

"Jules... she's crazy" He tries to get the phone away again and we engage in some wrestling. It feels excellent and when he's in just the right position, I tilt my pelvis up to his and slide it downward feeling his hardness. His eyes spark, eyebrows raising quickly. "It's nothing," I say.

"If it's nothing than you won't mind. . ." Laughing, Davis quickly pries the phone out of my hand and flops on his back beside me. *Don't leave. .. that was fun.*

I see Davis look at the text and I bite my lip.

HE'S GONNA MARRY YOU, YOU KNOW.

254

Davis throws the phone on the bedside table and is on top of me again in a flash. He is right back where I want him. He is looking at me so intently, it is beyond hot and I already have that heavy feeling in my lower belly and wetness between my legs. "See… I told you… Jules is crazy.."

He cuts me off sharply, "Lizard!" Then his face softens, his voice changes and he murmurs, "Biz. Jules… " Then breaking into a huge smile says, "Is RIGHT!"

My eyes and mouth open wide as I inhale. My hand comes up to my mouth at the same time.

It's a good thing I'm already lying down. . . .because he could have knocked me down with a feather.

Bonus: **Charlie Boxwood**

Man, I shoulda known when I showed them the picture, one of them woulda fallen for her. Biz. She had no idea how much people liked her. Completely unaware of how fucking cute and funny she could be. Smart assed. Inappropriate. Like a guy friend, but nothing like a guy friend 'cause she was so obliviously sexy. I told Jake and Davis all about her. How I felt bad 'bout how that guy fucked with her head last semester. How she was so quiet now, compared to last year.

I told'em straight up, "Man, when she's okay, she's a lot of fun. She was the coolest RA. We both worked part-time as bartenders at The Lum last year after we turned 21. We had read that book, you know, from the eighties? Less Than Zero. For modern lit class. Biz was always talking about how the movie wasn't nearly as good as the book. How Robert Downey, Jr. was awesome as Julian, but she just couldn't buy Andrew McCarthy. How she kept expecting him to say, "I Love You" in that really breathy voice and for Molly Ringwald to show up in a pink dress. Biz has a funny way of looking at things. After we read the book, we hatched a plan to save up all our tip money and buy cocaine and have non-stop sex, like in the book. That's right, me and Biz. Don't look so shocked. It coulda happened. But it didn't. We never bought the coke. And I only ever kissed her. When it happened we both agreed it was like kissing a sibling. So… sex would have been pointless. We just drank up our tips anyway and never saved anything. But planning it and talking about it for months—Fun. Shit, we laughed our asses off about it afterward. If that kiss had gone better, I bet we would have had a great time."

I don't know, it seems like Jake took my story as a challenge. To get the girl the bad guy had dumped.   To make himself out to be better at getting girls than me or any other guy. He sure fucked that up. Now, I have to find another damn guitarist for Boxwood. Jake sure as shit isn't getting near me or Jules or any of mine again. Especially Biz. We may have never hooked up, but now she's like a sister to me. Nobody fucks with my sister.

Davis was totally different. Davis saw that picture and said nothing. Just looked at it like he fell in love right in that moment. It was so weird. I had to drag him out of my room to go to rehearsal. I guess I knew one of them would wind up with her. Biz seems happier now, so I'm glad it's Davis, but I am not above going after him if he ever hurts her. In my gut, I get the feeling he won't.

Davis: Five Years Later

Hearing the front door close, I can finally breathe. I stop pacing and sit back on our bed, trying to recreate the relaxed position I was in earlier this evening. Propped up against a bunch of pillows with my legs out straight on top of the quilt. I throw my phone on the bedside table and mute CNN. I yell out to the hallway, "Hey Baby, you're back. How was it?" I haven't seen her face yet. Once I do, I'll know how it went, no matter what she tells me.

She walks into our bedroom and hangs her purse on the back of the desk chair. She tips her head to take off her stud earrings and tosses them into her jewelry box. I haven't seen her face yet.

259

"It was weird... at first... and then... fine. No drama." She

continues to remove her watch and is beginning to pull her t-shirt over

her head, when she finally turns to face me and give me a smile. I

have to admit, I'm distracted by the prospect of her t-shirt coming off.

It's been five years and I still get so turned on watching her undress.

The t-shirt comes off as she says, "He's...sweet." I don't like hearing

her say that. "and really a little sad. He's had two failed marriages

and no kids." I am holding back, but his sad life gives me satisfaction.

I know it shouldn't. I should be the bigger man. I just don't think I

will ever forget how he treated her. When he contacted her on

Facebook and asked her to "friend" him, we talked about it for a long

time. She is still so trusting and wants to believe the best in people.

Now that I think she finally believes the best about herself, she is less

vulnerable. So she friended him. Any time he talked to her through

the site, she shared it with me. He asked to meet her for coffee. I

wasn't happy about it, but it's her decision. I told her if she felt sad or

uncomfortable at any point to just get up and leave. If she felt scared

or unsafe to call me. I held my phone and paced in our bedroom the

entire time she was gone.

"He apologized about 20 times in the course of an hour. How he was so sorry if he hurt me. How he couldn't believe what an ass he was, cheating on me. All I could say was, 'Hey, it's fine. It was so long ago. Things are the way they are supposed to be now.' He shook his head like he didn't agree."

She has removed her capris and is walking around the room, throwing her clothes in the hamper and stretching a bit.

Staring at her, all I want to do is forget about her meeting with her ex, Jake. I want to make her forget it. All of it. It was difficult when she had to testify to send Neil to jail. She was so beautiful and brave through it all. If that OTHER guy, that motherfucking scum, Randall ever shows up again in her life, it will be a different story altogether. He's out there, evading arrest. I can never, ever forgive or forget what he did to her….or me. I push all thoughts of them out of my head and focus on Lizard.

"Jake still wants in your panties."

"What, these?" She turns her cute little ass toward me, looks over her shoulder and reaching around with her index fingers, snaps the bottom of both sides of her black boy shorts. That's it. I'm a goner. She moves to go toward our bathroom and I launch myself from my sitting position, grab her arm and not so gently pull her over to me. I am ready to go. "Grrr, It..Kills...Me...when you do that."

"Tell me about it, Mavis"

So I do. Three times.

Acknowledgments:

Thank you, Thank you, Thank you:

Sharon Korn, my Editor extraordinaire! You are truly The Cleaner. Thanks for taking care of my baby.

The awesome women of The Just Right Book Club. Your excitement and support helped me take the final leap.

My Beta readers: Cathy A. (my "Alpha" Beta), Linda, Brian, Kevin and Julie.

Anne Wathen, my legal consultant. Thanks for keeping me organized and legal.

And some amazing authors and book bloggers, I've never met in person, but who have inspired and helped me even if they didn't know it.

Jamie McGuire-for your FAQs for Writers page on your website. It saved me a lot of pain.

M. Leighton-tweeting with you helped me see that writers I love are just like me and spend time fooling around just like I do.

Jennifer Probst-you followed me on Twitter two minutes after I told the first person ever that I was writing a book. It felt like a sign. So I kept going.

Izzy at Fictional Boyfriends Facebook page-the first to ask for more info about BETTER THAN ME and Davis Brandon.

The supremely hilarious and inappropriate ladies of Book Boyfriend Reviews-Sandie, Dee and Shannon for doing a cover reveal for an unknown author.

Zoe at The Book Lover's Blog and Laura at Blame it on the Rain Blog. You are my UK Twitter girls. Thank you for the UK Cover Reveal.

And last-the loves of my life, BC and The Connor Boys. I swear I am buying t-shirts that say, "My Wife/Mother Writes Dirty Books," for you.

About the Author

Emme Burton is the author of Better Than Me, her debut novel. She lives in St. Louis, Missouri with her amazing husband, two teenage sons, and her "fur boy." Emme has never, ever been lost in a mall either as a child or an adult. Her mother, and now her family, have always known where to find her. At the bookstore.

Like Emme's Facebook Page: Author Emme Burton
And *Follow* her on Twitter: @EmmeBurton